# The Prophet of
# Rain

# The Prophet of Rain

*by*

*William Woodall*

*Jeremiah Press* · *Antoine, Arkansas*

Jeremiah Press
PO Box 121
Antoine, AR 71922
www.jeremiahpress.org

*First published by Jeremiah Press on 2/12/2008.*

*Printed in the United States of America.*

**This book is printed on acid-free paper.**

*ISBN 978-0-615-19236-9*

*Library of Congress Control Number: 2008922922*

*For Nathan, Elisabeth, and Mathew,*

*With much love. . .*

*This tale of dreams come true.*

# Contents

### *Chapter One*
### *Beginnings*

A long time ago, in a town beside a river, there lived a young boy named Jeremy, and he had red hair. Not like a carrot or an orange, but really the reddest you ever saw. . . red as apple peelings or rose petals, red as cherries in May. Now this might not have mattered much, after all, except for what came of it later, which I am just about to tell you.

On the day it all began, Jeremy would never have guessed that anything unusual was coming. He'd taken the cows down to drink from the river, as he usually did every evening when the sun had gone down a bit. It was a dull job most of the time. Now and then he had to prod one of the cows with a long stick to nudge her back onto the path, but that was all.

The distant shadow of the Cesmean Mountains lay ahead of him, and for a while Jeremy let his mind wander, imagining himself on the back of a wild stallion with a sword in his hand, tracking down and destroying the evil barbarians who were supposed to lurk there. He sighed, so quietly that he barely noticed it himself. There were so many things more exciting in the world than thirsty cows.

That sigh would have earned him a swift kick in the shins if his brother Melech had been with him that day. Melech was seventeen, and he didn't approve of daydreaming. Jeremy secretly thought it was because his brother was too stupid to imagine anything himself, but he would never have dared to say such a thing out loud. Melech would have smacked him for it.

The herd came to the top of the last rise in the path before it sloped steeply down to the nearly dry bed of the Murray River. The cool, heavy smell of water was in the air, and the cows trotted a little faster in their eagerness to reach it. Jeremy dawdled a while on the hilltop, shading his eyes from the low sun. The river trickled out of sight around a rocky outcrop not far to the west, and he knew that somewhere far away in that direction lay the sea, and the great city of Rustrum where King Joseph lived.

To the east, there was only the narrow valley climbing out of sight among the Eyre Hills. There was a gravelly sand bar at the foot of the path where useful things sometimes washed ashore, but no one knew where they came from. No one had ever gone that way to see.

He wondered what it might be like to start walking upstream, exploring the whole river until he found the place where it gushed out from the stone, or (it might be) flowed out from some deep and cold lake, high in the mountains. It might even be a magical lake that turned everything to gold, or contained an evil water dragon that nobody but he could ever kill. . . or maybe both! He smiled a little.

It is written, in the Book of the Prophets, that the Most High knows all the desires of our hearts, even the least wish of the most ignorant child. Such things are never passed by without answer, but the answer may often come in a form we never expected. So it was in this case.

Jeremy shook his head a little to collect his woolly thoughts. He noticed guiltily that several of the cows had finished drinking, and now they were drifting up and down the bank to graze. He hurried downstream to get ahead of the ones in that direction, a little annoyed with himself for not paying better attention. There might still be enough time to get them all home before anyone noticed it had taken him longer than it ought to. He hated the thought of seeing the smirk on Melech's face if anyone found out he'd let the cows wander off.

He ran carelessly in the gathering dusk, paying no attention to anything except the cows and what his brother would think of him for losing them. But greedy eyes watched him from the edge of the forest, and marked well that he was both young and alone. A caravan of Sohrab traders, passing by on business of their own, had decided to camp near the river for the night.

The Sohrab are an ancient people, and they had traded in rare and precious merchandise all up and down the Murray valley (and indeed, far beyond it), for time out of mind. They dealt in only the costliest and most difficult-to-find items. Jewels, spices, silks, the deep blue dye of Cerise, and, sometimes. . . slaves with flaming red hair. Anything unusual was always more valuable. Jeremy didn't realize his danger.

Just as he made it to the cow which had wandered farthest down the bank, he found himself quickly surrounded by tall men swathed in pale cotton robes. The Sohrab didn't come that way very often, but he recognized them at once. They looked unfriendly, with arms crossed silently and dark eyes that never blinked. He started to feel a little scared.

"Good evening, sirs. The village is that way," he said in a voice that he hoped sounded very polite and unafraid, and he raised his hand to point back upstream. One of the men nodded slightly, and Jeremy let himself relax a tiny bit. But when the man spoke, he felt real terror.

"You will come with us now, boy. You will fetch an excellent price in the mountains," the man said calmly, with a horrible smile.

Jeremy certainly didn't mean to give up without a fight, and he dashed for the riverbank as fast as he could go. It wasn't far to the edge of the water, and if he could swim to the opposite bank he might have enough time to hide among the trees that grew along the broken edge of the valley on that side. They would never find him there.

His speed caught them by surprise. He dodged easily through an opening in the circle of men, and hope surged through him as he saw the way open to the river. But luck was not with him that day (or maybe it was), and his foot caught on one of the bare roots trailing out from the edge of the forest. He stumbled, and even though he ran on for a little while, trying with all his might to regain his balance, he fell to the ground just at the water's edge. Before he could get back to his feet they were on him, pinning him to the ground harshly and crushing his face into the dirt. Someone kicked him in the ribs hard enough to knock the breath out of him, but the pain wasn't nearly so bad as the terror he felt.

They soon let him up, with a gag in his mouth to keep him from screaming for help, and from that moment on the traders made sure that at least two men held firmly to his arms at all times. He looked desperately for any chance to escape and hindered them as much as he was able, dragging his feet and going limp. He got a stinging slap in the face for that, and the men dragged him along the ground behind them anyway, not caring at all if the rocks tore his clothes and skin or if his arms got twisted.

They pulled him quickly to the Sohrab camp a little farther down the river, hidden carefully in the edge of the woods. The caravan was a small one, with six wagons drawn up in a rough circle against anyone who might be tempted to attack them. The Sohrab were known as vicious fighters when it came to protecting their merchandise, but there were still those who couldn't resist the lure of so much wealth. Jeremy was taken to one of the wagons, and put there alone in a sturdy cage of steel bars.   He immediately examined every corner and crevice to see if there might be any way out, but the Sohrab had built carefully.

Jeremy sat down in one of the corners, farthest back in the shadows, pulled his knees up to his chest, and buried his head in his arms.  His whole body hurt from being dragged across the river rocks, and his lip was bleeding a little.  He might have cried then, if he hadn't been so afraid.  He listened to the sounds of the camp outside, and guessed the Sohrab were getting ready to leave.  Probably so no one from the village could attempt a rescue.

Soon he was brought food and a flask of water, passed to him through the bars by one of the women whose task that was.  Jeremy chewed the bits of meat and cheese with no interest, hardly tasting them.  He wished bitterly that he'd listened to Melech and not daydreamed so much.  He wondered what had become of the cows, and how long it would be until someone came down to the river to look for him, and what they would think when they found him missing.  Would they wonder if a lion had killed him, or if he'd fallen in the river and drowned, or what?   He wondered what Melech would say.   Most of all, he wondered what these strange folk would do with him.  He knew they meant to sell him for a slave, somewhere, sometime, but that could mean many different things.

Jeremy curled into a ball in the corner of the cage against the creeping chill of the night, and then he did cry for a while. The gentle swaying of the wagon bed was soothing, and eventually, in spite of his fear, he slept.

### Chapter Two
### The House of Amagon

For the next several weeks, Jeremy rode in the cage. The Sohrab were not really very cruel to him; he was too valuable for that. They simply made sure he had no chance to escape. The caravan moved like a snail, but no one came to challenge them or to look for a missing boy. Or if they did, Jeremy heard nothing about it. For a while they had followed the Murray downstream, but after that they struck out in another direction entirely, and Jeremy had no idea where he might be. He was never allowed to see anything outside the wagon, except for a patch of sky above the back doors.    He was just as miserable as you might expect, even after he began to get used to the routine.

Sometimes one of the old women would sit in the wagon with him during the heat of the day, and out of loneliness he took to talking to her.  Not "with" her, for she never answered him, but she also never told him to be quiet.  So he told her about the village and the cows, and Melech and Papa, and his favorite dog, and playing ball on the village green with his friends. He told her about the lessons he remembered from the Book of the Prophets, and what he thought about them, and anything else that came to his mind.  She was a good listener, and he started to feel that she was his friend, in a strange sort of way.  For a while, he could almost forget he was locked in a steel cage on his way to a slave market, and then who knew what kind of horrors after that.  But Jeremy decided he would be patient for now, and see what happened.  There wasn't much else he could do until things changed.

After a few weeks, one of the Sohrab men came to his cage with a leather and steel collar for his neck, and a long steel chain attached to it.  Jeremy was made to wear this, and no amount of pulling and stretching could get it off.  From then on he was allowed to begin riding one of the smaller ponies during the day, with the end of his chain always attached to the belt of a man who rode beside him. They still put him in the cage at night, but it was a great improvement to be allowed outside even part of the time. He wasn't sure why the change was made. Jeremy could only guess at their reasons, for they never explained anything to him and never answered questions. Indeed, they hardly ever talked to him at all except to give orders, and that wasn't often. Whatever their purposes may have been, he was glad of them.

At first it was nice to feel the wind and the sun against his face after being locked up inside the stuffy wagon for so long, but soon he began to feel lonely again. He never saw the old woman anymore, and the Sohrab men expected him to be quiet. They weren't above enforcing it with blows if necessary, and Jeremy learned very quickly to keep his mouth shut.

The caravan traveled now through a country which had once been well settled, for the old stones that marked the edges of fields and vineyards still lined the road in places. It was all desolate and empty now, and dry as dust. Lack of rain had long since destroyed whatever people had once lived in that place. Even Jeremy's own village had not suffered so much, yet. Here there was no river to bring life-giving water to the parched fields and paddocks.

The Sohrab spent the night sometimes in the empty houses and barns when it happened to be convenient, but normally they didn't linger in these places. Jeremy guessed they had a civilized destination in mind, for all the wagons and packs were full of things to sell. He wondered again where they were taking him. The land was so vast and all so much the same that it was impossible for him to keep track of the road.

After weeks and weeks of travel through the dead farm country, the caravan went down through a deep cutting in a  cliff, and came out onto a well-kept road that ran along the banks of a river which, although low, still flowed strongly between banks of gray stone. They followed this road for some distance, and came eventually to a wide stone bridge that led across the river and into a great walled city, with blue pennants floating from the turrets on a soft warm breeze. The leader of the caravan halted at the gates, and after a whispered conversation with the gate guards, they were welcomed inside the city. The leader seemed to know exactly where to go, and soon the caravan came out into a wide stone plaza thronged with excited city folk. Within minutes, the Sohrab were set up to do business, with all their dazzling and costly merchandise displayed openly for the inspection of the city dwellers. Most turned away when they heard the prices, but there was still no shortage of those with plenty of gold to spend. By the end of the day, the Sohrab had raked in more money than Jeremy had ever dreamed existed in the world. Jeremy himself was put in a cage near the front of the Sohrab display, so customers could examine him better. Several did, even inspecting his teeth and looking at his feet and hands and feeling his muscles and asking how much he ate and whether he was good natured or not. This went on all day long, and still no one bought him. You can imagine what a nasty mood he was in by the time the market closed, after being poked and prodded for hours on end. He felt like biting the next person who wanted to look at his teeth.

Jeremy hoped, a little forlornly, that maybe they would let him go sooner or later if no one wanted to buy him. But the Sohrab are a crafty race, and they had never had any intention of selling him to anyone in the marketplace. Jeremy's buyer was already waiting; indeed, had already paid for him. The purpose of displaying him in the market was only to attract curiosity-seekers who might then be enticed to buy other items. Part of Jeremy's sale price had been the agreement that he was to remain in the cage all day for others to see. Jeremy knew nothing of that until much later, though.

Late in the evening three men came to the marketplace just as the Sohrab were packing their caravan to depart (for they never spent the night within the walls of a city), and with a deep bow, the leader of the caravan turned over the key to Jeremy's cage. Without a backward glance, the traders departed. Jeremy had to resist a strong urge to spit on the ground at them as they walked away.

Two of the servants picked him up, cage and all, and followed the third man to a large stone house somewhere in the city. He couldn't have said where it was in relation to the marketplace, for the streets were narrow and full of people. Nor did he suppose that it mattered much. The man who had bought him owned a stupendous palace, larger than any building Jeremy had yet seen within the city. It rose five stories high from the street, built of dressed gray stone, and had several towers and turrets that rose higher yet. There were no windows on the ground floor, but he could see a few in the upper reaches of the House. To his amazement, he saw that some of the upper windows were even made of glass, instead of the usual dried sheep skin or oiled paper. He couldn't imagine how rich the owner of the house must be, to afford so much glass. The double front doors were of stout beams of oak wood, reinforced with hinges of wrought iron.

Only one stood open, letting yellow lamplight spill out into the darkening street.

The door was so large that the servants easily carried Jeremy's cage through the opening. Inside was a grand atrium, paved with blue marble and with a stone fountain in the center. It was carved in the shape of a lion standing on a rock, and there had once been a pool of water all around the base of it, but that was dry now. Strange people dressed in blue silk and diamonds were moving to and fro across the room while he watched, but none of them seemed to pay any attention to him. Jeremy couldn't guess who they were or what they were doing.

He didn't have much time to look. The porters soon carried him to a grand staircase on the left side of the atrium, and then up several flights of stairs and along many lengthy passages until they came to a room inside one of the high stone towers that looked out over the rooftops of the city, with a glimpse of the dry land beyond. Here the servants set down the cage that held Jeremy, and all but one of them left the room. The one who remained locked the door quite carefully behind him, and then swung open Jeremy's cage and beckoned for him to come out.

Jeremy didn't need to be asked twice. He climbed out of the small door, stood up, and stretched his cramped body. The room he found himself in was just as richly furnished as the rest of the House. The walls and the floor were of blue veined marble, the furniture built of the rarest woods, inlaid with silver and upholstered with blue velvet. He noticed a low table set with golden dishes full of food, and a suit of new clothes, just his size, laid out fresh upon the velvet couch. He didn't know quite what to make of all this. In spite of his hunger, he stood still and looked silently at the man who had brought him, determined not to be the one to speak first.

"Please eat and refresh yourself, young master," the man said, gesturing toward the table. Jeremy couldn't tell for sure, but it was possible that the ghost of a smile had passed across his face. All the bitter fury he felt about his captivity threatened to boil up and overwhelm him, at the sight of that faint smile. But Jeremy had learned quickly among the Sohrab that caution was necessary, and he didn't lose his temper. It wouldn't do, and it might be very dangerous, to show any hint of anger toward this man. Still, he was determined to get some information, even if it did cost him a beating.

"Where am I?" he demanded finally. The old man did smile then, a warm smile that was very hard not to return. Jeremy found his anger and humiliation fading away a little in spite of himself.

"You are in the city of Cerise, in the House of Lord Amagon, and all will be well now that you're here, young man. Fear nothing, and be glad that you have come, for there are no slaves and no bondservants in the house of Amagon; only those who serve our Master in love and respect. And there are many such, for he is a great man. I am one of them, and I pray that you'll choose to stay here with us also. But first you must eat and bathe and refresh yourself, and dress as befits one of the household, for our Master wishes to talk with you as soon as you're ready," the old man said.

Jeremy was astonished at the sudden change in his fortunes, and he couldn't quite believe it. For a long moment he stood there with his mouth half open.

"And if I don't choose to stay?" he asked, suspiciously. The old man shrugged his shoulders, moved slowly to the door and unlocked it.

"There's the door, young master; you're free to go, if that's what you truly wish. As I said, there are no slaves and no prisoners in this house. But if you will stay just a little while, and speak to Lord Amagon. . . well, that's only courtesy to the one who purchased your freedom out of slavery among the Sohrab. Will you at least remain long enough to thank him?" the old man asked. Jeremy felt a little ashamed of himself, when things were put that way. It would be very rude and ungrateful not to thank the Master of the House, if that's the way things had happened. And if he could really leave whenever he wanted to, then maybe. . .

"I will speak to Lord Amagon," he said grudgingly. The old man smiled happily.

"Then please accept Lord Amagon's hospitality for this little while, young master. The bath is in the next chamber, and your clothes and various refreshments lie here before you. My name is Coreb, and I will await you in the hall outside. If you should require anything at all, simply call for me and I will do my best to provide it," he said.

Jeremy would really have liked to ask a lot more questions at that point, but Coreb vanished into the hallway with hardly more than a whisper of his shoes against the deep pile of the carpet, leaving Jeremy alone in the fancy room, with nothing for company but his own mightily confused thoughts.

He had been fully prepared to be surly and resistant to whatever he was ordered to do when he reached this place, and the courteous treatment he was getting left him befuddled and not sure how to act. He kept thinking there had to be a catch to all this, somewhere. But he was tired, and he was filthy, and caked in dirt and sweat, and he was ravenously hungry, and the means to correct all these things lay close at hand. He decided for the time being at least he would take things at face value.

Accordingly, he entered the next chamber, stripped off his dirty rags, and slipped gratefully into the marble basin of the bath. It was the first time in weeks that he'd had the luxury of a bath, and the simple pleasure of being truly clean again improved his mood immensely. There were various bath oils and soaps arranged around the tub, and a seemingly limitless supply of hot and cold water. Jeremy scrubbed himself thoroughly until his skin was pink and glowing, and his hair restored to its normal deep red. After drying himself with one of the thick white towels and combing his hair, he returned to the other room and put on the clothes laid out for him on the couch. There was a white linen shirt and pants, and a long blue robe of watered silk that came down to his ankles, hemmed and bordered with white gold and diamonds. The shoes were soft blue leather and curled up at the toes. Everything was wonderfully soft and comfortable, not at all as you might expect nice clothes to be. They were almost as nice to wear as they were to look at. Jeremy couldn't resist going to the large mirror on the wall to see himself, and couldn't help laughing at his reflection.

He'd never looked so strange in all his life, he thought. Then he quickly returned to the table and attacked the food that had been left for him. At first he was too hungry to care much what it tasted like and he paid close attention to business, but as his hunger subsided a bit he realized he'd never tasted such a meal before. There were iced fruits, and fresh white bread with butter, and toasted bits of meat and cheese with tangy sauces. He began to eat more slowly, so as to savor it all more thoroughly. At that point he was feeling quite kindly toward his host, and well disposed to listen to whatever he had to say. Coreb seemed to appear out of thin air, and stood by the door.

"Are you ready, young master?" he asked. Jeremy was, and together they left the room in the tower. Coreb led him through many other halls and passageways, full of tapestries and golden candle sconces and crystal and paintings, until he was dizzy with the size of the place. At last they arrived in a room somewhat plainer than the others; not very large, and containing only a wooden table and two chairs. In one of them sat a young man, tall and fair of face, with dark hair and bright blue eyes. He was dressed all in blue, with only a small handful of diamonds to adorn his clothes. Fewer than Jeremy wore, in fact. He was reading a book, and looked up when Coreb opened the door. He smiled at them both.

"I'm glad to see you looking so well, young man," he said to Jeremy, and waved a hand for him to sit down and for Coreb to leave them alone. Jeremy took the other chair and quietly watched Lord Amagon. Strangely, it was the book which impressed him more than the wealth. The wealth meant nothing to him, because he didn't really comprehend its value yet. But in the village, the only book that existed was a copy of the Book of the Prophets, and that was always kept in the church. Not many people could have read it, even if there had been a copy in every house. The priest could read, and maybe one or two others, but few took the time to learn more than the small amount that was necessary for everyday tasks. The fact that Amagon knew how to read raised him a good bit in Jeremy's respect. He wasn't at all the sort of fellow Jeremy had expected.

"So, tell me, young man, what's your name?" Lord Amagon asked.

"Jeremy," the boy said. Lord Amagon smiled and shook his hand.

"And do you know, Jeremy, why you're here, and why I purchased your freedom from the Sohrab?"

"No, sir, I don't," Jeremy admitted.

"Well, then, I'll tell you," Lord Amagon said, laying his book aside and sitting more comfortably in his chair.

"Perhaps, if you've noticed much of my home as you walked to and fro, you may have seen that I have been blessed with a great deal of wealth. Indeed, I am quite likely the wealthiest man in all the kingdom, if not the world. Perhaps you've heard of the blue dye of Cerise, which is the costliest and rarest in the world, and which is sold only to kings and noblemen. That dye comes from a mine in the hills nearby, and I am the owner of that mine. I have the means to do a great many things for my city, and for those who happen to cross my path from time to time. I keep on good terms with the Sohrab, for it is impossible to trade in any merchandise without taking them into account. Some of them I know quite well, and it happens that one of these I know is an old caravan leader and his wife, who trade on the eastern marches."

"It's been useful for me to know them, for sometimes they come across items of great value, which they naturally wish to offer to me, first. You are one such item, though perhaps they never would have realized it, if you hadn't been so talkative." Here Amagon smiled.

"You may not know how much time you spent talking to the leader's wife, but she was very impressed with you. As soon as the caravan drew near to Cerise, she and her husband came to me, and told me they had something special that might interest me. They had intended to sell you to one of the chieftains of the Lachishite barbarians in the mountains, for those are an ignorant and superstitious folk, and red is a sacred color to them. I'm not sure what they would have done with you. . . maybe kept you for a luck charm, or married you off to one of their girls, or they might have bled you now and then and drunk your blood because they thought it was specially holy, or some other barbaric and brutal thing like that. The Sohrab would not have cared what became of you, after cash was in hand. Make no mistake. . . they know I keep no slaves, but to them it matters not at all what a customer chooses to do with the things he buys, so long as they get their payment. In any case, the old lady told me you are both intelligent and good of heart, and these are things I have much need of, in my various dealings."

Amagon paused for a moment, and looked at Jeremy frankly.

"And also. . . though some may consider it foolish, I couldn't allow a child of my own people to be condemned to a lifetime of slavery (or worse) among the Lachishites. Not if I knew of it in time, and if it lay within my power to prevent it."

"And so it is that I have purchased your freedom. You may take it and go, if you wish, but I must for the sake of mercy warn you that another Sohrab clan would be quite happy to recapture you and sell you again, perhaps to someone less considerate than myself. I'm not on such good terms with every caravan, and I can affect little that goes on beyond Cerise. However, if you wish, you may remain here in my house to serve me. You will be provided with clothes, and quarters, and all that you require, and I will pay you a good wage, as I do all my servants. What do you think of my offer?" Lord Amagon asked.

Jeremy saw at once that he had no real choice. The Sohrab awaited him outside the city walls, and that alone turned the offer of freedom into a mockery. But still. . . Lord Amagon didn't have to offer him anything. In time something better might turn up, but for now he could think of no better plan for himself.

"I accept your offer, sir," he said.

## Chapter Three
### *Jonah*

"Excellent," Lord Amagon said. "For now, I will make you a page. It will be your duty to deliver messages to various places in the city or beyond, at such times as I or others in the house may require. I don't think you will find the work difficult, after you have learned your way around the streets. However, you will also be expected to learn to read and write, and to speak certain useful languages, and to practice courtesy, and such other things as are needful for a noble and gentle person to know. When you are not occupied with these tasks, your time is your own, but you are expected to return to the House no later than sundown each day, unless you are told otherwise. If you don't, you may find yourself locked outside for the night."

Lord Amagon clapped his hands, and Coreb instantly appeared from outside the doorway.

"Coreb, take this boy to the pages' barracks, and ensure that he has all things needful," Amagon ordered.

"Of course, sir," Coreb replied, with a deep bow. Before leaving the room with Coreb, Jeremy looked back at Amagon for a moment.

"Thank you, sir," he said sincerely. Amagon smiled.

"Thank the Most High, and not His humble servant," he said. Jeremy had never heard anyone but a priest say such a thing before, and his impression of Lord Amagon went up yet another notch.

Coreb led him back down into the main part of the House, all the way to the ground floor. They didn't go by way of the grand staircase that would have brought them back to the front atrium, but somehow arrived at the rear of the House not far from what must have been the kitchen. Jeremy could hear pots and pans being washed up, and the lingering odor of bread and roast meat filled the air. He was hopelessly lost, but he supposed he would learn his way around soon enough. Some distance down the hall from the kitchen, they came to a smaller set of double doors that stood ajar, and Coreb led him into the barracks.

It was a long room, containing thirty bunks along the inside wall, with a wardrobe or cabinet of sorts beside each one. Across from the beds were large glass windows that looked out onto the herb-and-vegetable garden used by the kitchen. The entire House was built around a central courtyard, to which there was no access except by passing through the House itself. The ground floor rooms which faced the courtyard could safely have windows, for no enemy could approach from that direction anyway. Across the garden and the rest of the courtyard were other parts of the House, but Jeremy couldn't tell what they might be in the semi-darkness.

There were about twenty other boys in the room when they arrived. . . resting on their bunks, reading, talking to each other, or playing games at one of the wooden tables by the windows. They were of various ages, from slightly younger than Jeremy all the way up to tall youths with thin beards. They all looked up when Coreb appeared at the door.

"Boys, this is Jeremy, who will be joining you. Please make him feel welcome," Coreb said. This was met with a loud chorus of greetings. Jeremy smiled, a little uncertainly.

Coreb took Jeremy to the bunk nearest the door and showed him the contents of his locker- five sets of uniforms, a nicer suit of clothes much like the ones he was wearing, to be used on feast days or for chapel services, and two sets of plain cotton jumpers for dirty or difficult work. There were also boots and caps and other necessary things. When all this was done, Coreb excused himself, reminded the boys that it would be time for lights-out soon, and shut the door.

There were in fact twenty-three other pages at the time Jeremy came to the House. They were friendly and seemed to like each other, but Jeremy never felt that he had much in common with them. They were mostly the younger sons of wealthy families in Cerise. Not one of them had ever set foot outside the city walls nor ever suffered a day of want. Jeremy couldn't help thinking of them as overgrown babies. . . even the older boys who shaved twice a week. This put up a subtle wall between them, so that Jeremy never made any real friends among the other pages. He worked well with them, and even played and talked with them, but he was close to no one.

Time passed, and life was not unkind to him. He did his work well and without complaint, as he'd always been taught to do, and he watched his pay accumulate in the bank downtown. He had nice things, and a respected place in the House. He was taught to read and cipher, and studied geography and music and many other things he could never have learned in the village of his birth. Cerise was a beautiful and interesting city, with many things to see and do. He liked to walk down to the stone-paved marketplace on Sunday afternoons and watch the jugglers and the bear tamers who gathered there, and it was sometimes possible to see traders who brought merchandise from the farthest corners of the world. He avoided the marketplace whenever a caravan of Sohrab came to trade, for he could never quite forget the horror of his captivity with them and he disliked being reminded of it. But they didn't come often, and there were many other traders besides them. Jeremy had no real complaints about his life, except for a vague sort of loneliness. He wasn't used to spending so much of his time alone. Melech had been hateful sometimes, but at least he was always there. Or if not, then Jeremy had always had friends to do things with. Here there was no one except the other pages, and try as he might, he found it awfully hard to take them seriously.

On a cold day in the winter, when he'd been in the House for several months, it happened that Jeremy found himself with nothing to do. No messages needed to be sent, and his studies were done for the day. All the other pages were busy, and it was much too cold to think of going out. He hung around the kitchen for a while to see if he could scrounge something to eat, but eventually the cooks shooed him away. He soon got tired of sitting by the fountain. With nothing else to do, he decided to take a lamp and explore the House for a while. No matter how much he roamed the halls, there always seemed to be more of it to see.

On this day, he eventually came out in the stable where the horses were kept. This was a place he'd never had any reason to visit before, so he took some passing interest in it.

The stable boys were in the middle of grooming the horses when he arrived, for Amagon expected his mounts to look presentable at all times. Jeremy knew lots about cows, but the only horses in the village had been a couple of old draft animals that were used to plow the fields. No one rode, and certainly there were no such beautiful animals as these. Jeremy sat down on an upended water bucket and watched the stable boys work for a while.

The boy nearest him was younger than the others, working with a curry comb on a chestnut horse nearly twice his height. Even with a stool, he was having trouble reaching all the way up onto the horse's withers. He had the jet black hair and bright blue eyes of almost all the people of Cerise. . . a combination Jeremy was still not quite used to.

"Could I help?" Jeremy finally asked, after watching the boy for a while. The boy turned to him with a ready smile.

"It's not so easy as it looks, I'm afraid. But if you like, I'll teach you how," he said.

"Sure," Jeremy said, getting up from the bucket and walking into the stall.

Jonah (for that was the boy's name) turned out to be a fun and friendly person to talk to. He made himself old friends with Jeremy at once, as if they'd known each other for years instead of just met. He tried to show the older boy how to curry the horse, but it soon became obvious he was trying hard not to laugh as he watched.

"Here, you better let me finish her," Jonah finally said, smiling. Somehow Jeremy didn't mind being laughed at. It reminded him of playing with his friends in the village, when everybody knew the laughter was good-natured. So he laughed a little himself, and handed back the comb.

"You're right, it's harder than it looks," he admitted, "How did you learn how to do it so well?"

"Aw, I've been doing this since I was old enough to hold a comb in my hands," Jonah told him.

"You've been here that long?" Jeremy asked.

"No, no. . . I've only been here in the House about three months.  But I grew up on a horse farm outside the city.  All my family knows about horses," he said proudly.

"I wish I did, but we only had cows," Jeremy said wistfully.

They went on talking for quite a while, and when he finished grooming the horse Jonah was done with work for the day.  He carefully put away his brushes and tools, patted the horse on her flank, and then dusted his hands and looked at Jeremy.

"If you're not doing anything, would you like to come up to the loft and play darts?" he asked, as if just thinking of it.

"Sure," Jeremy said.  He followed Jonah up a wooden ladder to the hay loft above the stable.  The stable boys had cleared out a small area for a table and chairs, and there was a dart board against one wall.  They were surrounded by walls of golden and sweet-smelling hay that reached right up to the roof.

"All this will be gone by springtime," Jonah said, waving an arm at the hay. It didn't seem possible to Jeremy that the horses could ever eat that much. . . but he supposed some of it was used for bedding and other things too.

"How do you get it all up here?" he asked, since he was sure it didn't come up and down the ladder.

"Oh, there's a big trap door way down at the far end. We use that for getting the hay in and out when we need to. The ladder is just for getting up here to our little dart place, mostly," Jonah explained.

They played several games of darts, until the winter sun began to fade. Lamps or candles of any kind were strictly forbidden in the hay loft because of the danger of fire, and so the end of daylight also meant the end of their games. Jonah was a much better dart player, but Jeremy enjoyed himself anyway. After supper in the Great Hall, they agreed to meet in the hay loft and play some more the next afternoon.

The two of them soon became fast friends. Jonah had less free time than Jeremy did, but on Sundays and some evenings, when the weather was nice, they left the House together and explored Cerise. Jonah's favorite activity was to go up on the city wall and flick peanut shells down onto the heads of people leaving the city through the gate. He was very skilled at this, and soon taught Jeremy to do it almost as well as he did. Sometimes the victims looked up at the battlements and laughed, and sometimes they scowled or cursed at the boys. Jonah had come to the wall many times and already had a fair idea who the sourpusses were, and generally they tried to aim for the ones who would laugh.

Jeremy took them to the marketplace to watch the dancing bears and the traders, and other times they just roamed the streets together, seeing whatever there was to see. Neither of them knew much about the city. Jeremy had arrived in a cage, and Jonah had never set foot within the walls until the day he came to Lord Amagon's stables.

"Do you like it here, Jonah?" Jeremy asked his friend one day, as they sat on the wall. They were not flicking peanut shells today, just enjoying the cooler wind atop the battlements. There were several picnickers and strollers with the same idea. It was high summer, and the heat rising from the pavement stones on the street was almost unbearable.

"It's as good as may be," Jonah shrugged. "I don't want to do it for always, but I like the House and I like the City, and the other boys in the stable are nice fellows to work with."

"Oh, I know. It's a good place like that. But what do you want to do when you leave here?" Jeremy asked.

"Be King of Rustrum and do anything I please, of course," Jonah laughed. He reached over and punched Jeremy's arm in a friendly sort of way. "Why are you asking me all this, anyway?"

Jeremy chewed on his lip and thought about that a while.

"I don't know. I've been trying to think about what I might do when I get too old to be a page anymore. The pagemaster always tells us to plan ahead like that, so I guess I'm just curious about what other people are thinking about," he said at last. Jonah rolled his eyes.

"You're too darned serious, Jeremy. That's years and years away," he said.

"True, but I just wonder sometimes," Jeremy said.

"Well, I'll tell you what I think, since it matters so much to you. I hope I can become a scholar at the university, and find out all kinds of things nobody ever knew before. And I hope I can do something for my family back in the village, maybe," Jonah said, soberly.

Jeremy thought about this.

"I'm not sure what I want," he said quietly. "I want to do something noble and grand, you know. Kill a dragon like they used to do in the old days, or explore a huge desert on foot, or swim across the sea and find out what's on the other side of it. Something wild and awesome like that."

Jonah looked at his friend for a second as if not sure what to say, then he laughed a little and punched his arm again.

"Now I know you're crazy, boy," he said, not unkindly. After a second Jeremy laughed too, and the serious topic was forgotten.

Jonah, when he wasn't being a prankster, was generally a trustworthy and respectable boy. He knew lots of interesting things, and he didn't mind sharing what he knew. He taught Jeremy how to ride the horses properly (his short experience of riding with the Sohrab caravan hardly counted), and sometimes they would ride out through the gates and around the countryside. It was good for the horses to get exercised regularly, and Lord Amagon didn't mind if the stable boys left the city from time to time, provided they didn't go too far and treated the horses well.

Most of the area close to Cerise was farm land watered by ditches dug from the Blue River, with patches of oak woods here and there. The main road led beside the riverbank- north to the dye mines, and far south to Rustrum. The old east road led up onto the High Plain and the Eyre Hills (and finally to Jeremy's village) but that way wasn't used much anymore. The boys generally stuck to the main road by the river, for there was more to see and do that way. They sometimes went to Jonah's village, three miles upstream. There was a deep, wide pool in the river at that place, with huge willow trees leaning far out over the water, and in the summertime they could tie up the horses and go swimming. Jeremy was as good a swimmer as Jonah was, for Melech had taught him to swim almost before he could walk. It was one of the few kind things he could ever remember his brother doing.

Jeremy wouldn't have wanted to go home now even if he could have. He had a much better life in Cerise than he could ever have hoped for in the village, and he knew he wasn't the first boy who ever had to find work in a distant city. If Papa had been able to find a tradesman to apprentice him to, he might have had to leave home soon anyway, Sohrab or not. He knew all this in his mind, but there were still times when he missed his old life more than he would have believed possible. He didn't say much about it, most of the time. Jonah usually knew what he was thinking at times like that, and for once didn't tease him about being too serious. He knew what it felt like to leave home, too.

Jonah could still go back and visit his family now and then, though. He asked Jeremy to come with him whenever he went, and Jeremy soon discovered that he enjoyed these visits very much. They were kindly folk, though not quite what he was used to. Jonah had at least twelve brothers and sisters, some older and some younger. They all lived in a three room wooden house surrounded by wide pastures for horses, and Jonah's two older brothers were expert horsemen. One of his sisters was already married, but she still lived nearby and even brought her own baby to the house as often as not. The place always seemed on the very verge of bursting with people. They were a family that joked and laughed a lot, and nothing ever seemed to annoy or upset them. They took Jeremy to heart like a long-lost son and brother, from the moment he first walked in the door, without even thinking about it. Jeremy might have been surprised by this, if he hadn't already seen it from Jonah himself. As it was, he sometimes felt more at home in that house than he ever had in the place he was born to. He felt a little disloyal for that, but he couldn't help it.

Jonah sometimes laughed and said he hadn't known he was getting another brother, but he meant it kindly.

Jeremy never did learn to be more than a decent rider, but he had lots of fun in the process. He was happier in those days than he could ever remember, and he thanked the Most High every day for bringing him to Cerise. He would certainly never have come there without the Sohrab, and he could even be thankful for his captivity, when he thought about it.

One glad day followed another, until he began to believe those times would go on forever. But of happy days and golden years there is often little to say, while they last. Nor do they last forever, in a dark and fallen world.

For the rest of his life, Jeremy never forgot those years in Cerise, and the memory of joy stood him in good stead during the evil days that lay ahead.

## *Chapter Four*
### *Eli*

After three years, Jeremy was placed over all the pages in the household, so high had he risen in the favor of Lord Amagon. The position was an important one, for all of Amagon's messages and the smooth running of his day-to-day life depended on the pages. It was a high honor for one so young. Most of the time Jeremy loved his work, but as time went on he gradually began to feel unsatisfied again. There was little challenge to be faced, little to be done which seemed awesome or grand. He couldn't quite put his finger on what it was he wanted. . . it was just something that nagged him in the back of his mind, like an itch he couldn't quite scratch. There were times when he thought it might drive him crazy, and when he had these moods he became irritable and restless. No amount of honor and money could ever quite kill the desire for greatness that was written on his heart.

He took to walking the streets of the city alone, deep in thought. If he stayed in the House, there were always people who needed to see him about something or other, and he wanted time to think. His wanderings took him into places he'd never visited as a page boy, for there was little need to send messages to the poorer sections of town. Old clothes and a droopy hood over his head helped to make him less recognizable, for he knew it wouldn't do at all to be known as a servant of one of the great Houses. At best it would make people uneasy, and at worst it might earn him a cut throat in a dark alley. Parts of the city were very dangerous territory, and he couldn't have said why he felt compelled to visit such places. He didn't often do much except watch people, and sometimes talk to them. He knew Lord Amagon and even Jonah would have been horrified if they knew where he'd been. So he kept his roaming to himself, and said nothing about his restless thoughts.

It chanced that on one of these walks, he ended up near the River Gate on the east side of the city. . .

not a very safe place to be, with night approaching. The narrow street was fronted with cheap taverns with names like *The Little Brown Jug* or *The Blood and Guts*. The muddy filth on the streets stuck to the bottom of his shoes, for the paving stones were rarely washed in this neighborhood. He watched a barefoot old woman in a dirty skirt digging through a trash pile beside one of the taverns, and heard the not-too-distant sound of drunk men fighting. It was a sad place, and Jeremy had almost made up his mind to turn around and go home.

Almost, until he saw a young boy huddled against a trash pile, with a little cup in front of him to beg for coins. There were many like him in the back alleys of Cerise, but today Jeremy felt an impulse to talk to this one. The boy looked up at him as he approached. This was a little unusual, for most beggars kept their heads down and didn't dare look into the eyes of the city folk. The boy was thin and ragged and filthy, with the dull eyes that came from hunger and lack of love. Jeremy squatted down so as to speak to him more easily.

"What's your name, boy?" he asked.

"My name is Eli, may it please your grace," the boy said. That also was unusual, for the boy's speech was unlike that of an ignorant street urchin. Noblemen and cultured folk addressed one another in that fashion, if they were roughly equals, but it was unheard of to be called "your grace" by a child, much less a street beggar. Indeed it could even be taken as an insult, if the boy had only known it. He obviously did not, so Jeremy let it pass. He was curious enough to ask about it, though.

"Tell me, Eli, how is it that you speak to me as an equal?" he asked mildly. He didn't mean this in a harsh way, for he was simply curious. But his words struck terror into the child.

"I'm sorry, lord! I meant no offense!" he cried, cringing down on the filthy street and dropping his face as if he expected a blow. Jeremy hastily reached down and pulled the boy's face up to look at him again.

"I'm not offended, Eli. . . I'd just like to know why you called me 'your grace'," he explained, as calmly as he could. The boy couldn't answer him for few minutes until he had gotten over his fright.

"Lord, I found the words in a book of old tales. I meant only to do you honor," he said.

"You can read?" Jeremy asked, more than a little shocked.

"Yes, Lord, but only a little. The old priest at the church by the River Gate taught me a little, before he died," the boy said.

Jeremy thought about this for a long time. It must have been an awfully kind and devoted priest, to have taken the time to do such a thing. Jeremy wished for a minute that he knew the man's name. Then he looked at the child more carefully, for he had the beginnings of an idea.

"Do you have a family, Eli?" he asked.

"No, Lord. My sister died of the fever three months ago, and she was the last," Eli said.

"And how old might you be?" Jeremy wanted to know.

"Thirteen years, Lord," the boy replied promptly. Jeremy would never have guessed it, for the boy was very small for his age, but he saw no reason not to believe him.

Jeremy quickly made a decision.

"Eli, would you like to leave this place, and live in a great House, and work an honest job, and never beg again?" he asked. This was a calculated risk. He was pagemaster, and one of his duties was to choose and train the youngsters who did that job in the House, but it was unheard of for a great Lord to pick his servants from among the beggars on the street. Jeremy wasn't entirely sure Lord Amagon would approve of what he was doing. Nor was he certain the boy himself would accept the offer. His heart would have to be still soft enough to trust that the chance was real, and that he must really try his best to make it work. Most boys who lived on the street wouldn't have believed it, and would have tried only to steal as much from the House as they could before the chance slipped away. Jeremy honestly didn't know what Eli would do.

The younger boy said nothing for a few minutes, then looked up at Jeremy with clear blue eyes.

"Lord, I would give anything to have a life like that," he said.

"Then will you come with me to my master's House, and always do your best?" Jeremy asked, and held his breath.

"Yes, Lord. I'll come with you," Eli agreed.

"Excellent!" Jeremy exclaimed. "Come with me."

He reached down and took Eli's hand, and led him back through the narrow streets to Lord Amagon's House. Jeremy was soon sorry he'd taken the boy's hand, for he stank like rotten garbage and old sweat. Long before they reached the House, Jeremy was breathing as shallowly as possible, trying not to gag and embarrass the boy. When they got within a few blocks of the House, he began to wonder how he could ever get Eli inside, filthy and stinking as he was. It was too late to find a public pump and wash him off, for the sun would soon be down, and Jeremy had no intention of being locked outside all night. After some thought, he went to the little kitchen door where vegetables and things were brought in, instead of going to the front doors that would have led into the grand atrium. He hoped they might attract less attention that way.

No such luck. Jeremy was the object of shocked glances and even a gasp or two when he entered the House with a street beggar, but none of the cooks dared question him about the matter. He took a fresh loaf from the cooling tray above the oven to give to Eli, after he noticed the boy looking hungrily at the food.

"Eat slowly," Jeremy cautioned. He wasn't sure when Eli had last eaten, and he didn't want the boy to gorge on the food and then throw up because he ate too fast. Eli nibbled his bread obediently as they entered the quieter parts of the House, and Jeremy took him to the page barracks. It was deserted at that hour, for all the boys had gone to supper in the Great Hall.

Jeremy collected robes and shoes while Eli had a proper bath. It was a lengthy one, because he was so filthy the water had to be changed twice before he was done. Jeremy had to show him how to dress in the clothes of the House, and finally it was necessary to assign him a bunk.

Jeremy had changed things since the days when he himself had first come to the House. Now, only about six of the youngest boys lived together in the barracks. After a boy had been in the House for a year, and if he proved himself worthy of more responsibility, then he was given a private room nearby. Those whose work was less than pleasing were moved to a separate barracks hall for another year. If they failed to improve even after that, they were dismissed from the House and replaced. This system of rewards was very popular with the pages, especially with the ones who worked hard, and the messenger service had quickly become more efficient than ever before. Jeremy himself had an apartment of four rooms on the second floor, but still not far from the barracks. He liked to be close by in case he was needed.

"If you should need anything, or if you have questions, ask one of the other pages, or tell them to send for me. But for now, it will soon be time for bed, and tomorrow you'll have many things to begin to learn. I'll expect to see you, properly dressed and with your bunk made up, no later than eight o'clock. Understood?" Jeremy asked.

"Thank you, sir," Eli said, and kissed Jeremy's sapphire signet ring after the manner of the old-fashioned folk of Cerise. It was another custom that wasn't exactly proper under the circumstances, this time because Jeremy didn't rank high enough. It was the sort of thing one might do when giving honor to high nobles and royalty on ceremonious occasions. Eli had been reading too many fairy tales, and his idea of proper courtesy was imperfect to say the least. Jeremy was afraid the boy was going to get seriously laughed at until he learned better. But in the meantime, it was much better to have imperfect manners than none at all.

Over the next few weeks, Eli turned out to have been a good choice for the House. For the most part. He always kept a slightly scrappy temper from his time on the streets, and he soon earned a respectable reputation as a fighter, even against boys much bigger than himself. Those who were inclined to laugh at his rough accent or his strange manners quickly learned to keep such thoughts to themselves. Eli never fought in the House itself or under any circumstances that might embarrass Lord Amagon, and so Jeremy officially pretended not to notice. In time, the problem faded.

Jeremy was very pleased that Eli had worked out so well, and from that day forward, for as long as he remained in the House of Amagon, he continued the habit of giving a place in the House to such promising boys as he found on the streets.

This didn't always work out. Some of the boys were thieves or worse, but Jeremy didn't allow that to discourage him. A handful of the street boys became good and faithful servants, and he was willing to endure the problems the bad boys brought him, for the sake of the few good ones who had no other chance in the world. Lord Amagon was well pleased with Jeremy's project.

He didn't realize it at the time, but Jeremy's work among the street boys earned him a great deal of love from the common people, for no Lord had ever taken such an interest in them before. And that turned out well indeed for him, later on.

Soon after this, Jonah came to him and asked for a place in the messenger service, for the work was pleasanter and more interesting than stable boy, with more time to study. Jeremy was glad to help him, for Jonah was still his closest friend. Jonah needed little training to make the switch, since he'd already spent so much of his free time studying even while he worked in the stable. Still, Jeremy was obliged to send him to the beginner's barracks, so as not to unfairly favor him. Jonah didn't really like the idea of spending a whole year with boys two or three years younger than himself, but he was willing to accept the necessity if he had to.

As it happened, Jonah's sunny personality made him a popular leader among the younger boys, and he enjoyed his time there more than he had expected he would. He became friends with all the younglings, in fact, especially Eli and another boy named Daniel.

Daniel was the youngest boy in the House at the time, only twelve, and anyone more unlike Jonah could hardly be imagined. He was quiet, didn't laugh much, and was so soft hearted that Jeremy had once seen him stop in the middle of the street to pick up worms off the pavement to keep them from being stepped on. Aside from that, Jeremy could remember only that he was the middle son of a minor city official. Jeremy knew all the pages to some extent, but some he knew much better than others. Daniel was easy to overlook.

In a way, Jeremy wasn't surprised that Jonah had become so popular with the youngsters. He was like that with everybody. He had friends all over the city, both young and old, rich and poor, of every stripe and kind. Everyone loved him, and Jeremy sometimes envied him for the easy way he got along with people. He wondered if Jonah had ever taken Eli and Daniel to flick peanut shells off the city walls. The thought made him laugh.

Jeremy soon had no time to wonder what Jonah was doing, though. All during that spring and summer, Lord Amagon gradually began spending more and more time away from the House, sometimes for long periods, and Jeremy was usually the one left in charge at those times. He was soon given his own key to the front doors, for the Master trusted no one else to manage things while he was gone. Jeremy would have appreciated the honor more, if he hadn't been so worried about the circumstances. Amagon would never say where he'd been or what he was doing, and he often had an anxious frown on his face when he thought no one was looking. There were even times when he slipped out the kitchen door late at night in disguise, and Jeremy was told to keep up the pretense that the Master was still in the House. This was very difficult, for there were always people who wanted to see Lord Amagon, and some of them were hard to turn away. Merchants and casual visitors were one thing, but what could he say to a messenger from the Satrap or the Captain of the Guard? Such people were not used to being refused. It became almost impossible to go on pretending when these periods went on for several days or even weeks at a time.

This uneasy situation continued for many months, and Lord Amagon's mood and strange behavior began to cast a dark cloud over the House. Even the youngest kitchen girl began to notice that something wasn't quite right. By the time summer was ending, Jeremy was very nearly running the House all the time, for Amagon didn't seem interested in such things anymore even when he was home. It was a heavy burden for Jeremy, especially since he couldn't discuss it with anybody.

There was worse to come. As head of the messenger service he began to hear frightening rumors about treachery against the King and secret plans to overthrow him. Such talk was being whispered in the great Houses of Cerise, and sooner or later all rumors of that kind made their way to the ears of the King. Then death would come swiftly to anyone whose name was mentioned in connection with such a rumor, whether guilty or not. The King was known to be cruelly harsh with anyone who threatened his power, or even seemed to.

Jeremy was afraid serious trouble was coming, and he dearly hoped Lord Amagon wasn't involved with any such scheme. Especially not one with such careless conspirators. He felt in his bones that things were getting dangerous, and he decided to speak to the Master at the very first opportunity.

## Chapter Five
### Treachery

There were other reasons to have a serious talk with the Master as well, and chief among them was the continuing drought. It had been twenty-three years since the rain last fell on Cerise, and even longer than that in some places. All across the length and breadth of the land people and beasts were dying of thirst. Only the deepest wells continued to give any water to the desolate land. Even the Blue River and the Murray were at last beginning to run dry, and soon there would be nothing left to drink or grow crops. The members of Lord Amagon's House had not suffered very much yet, for their Master had the money to pay for water and food, but Jeremy knew that couldn't go on forever. All the money in the world couldn't buy what didn't exist, and it was getting dangerously near that point. Others were not so fortunate, and the Satrap had put the entire city on a daily water ration of only a gallon per family, except for those who could pay a steep price for extra. News came from Rustrum that the King had ordered a gathering of all his wisest councilors, to advise him on how the drought might be ended.

Now Joseph had been a wicked King, from all that Jeremy had ever heard of him. The doings and the people of Rustrum had never had much effect on the herders of the upper valleys, except when the tax collectors came. Jeremy's village had always paid one cow every year, which had never seemed like much. It was possible to lose more than that to wild dogs or thieves every year. So the people had paid little attention to the King, but even in the village gossip had been heard sometimes. Of how the King had accepted bribes when he dealt with those who came to him for justice, and of his greed and cruelty with the people of the lowlands.

Since coming to Cerise, Jeremy had heard even worse things. It was whispered that the King had gone to worship in the groves of Marithe and Cesme as the drought continued, and drunk sacred blood after the manner of the Lachishite barbarians, and thus blasphemed the name of the Most High. Jeremy was amazed that the King had not already been struck dead by fire from heaven, if such things were true. But who could tell? Whispers were just that- whispers, and only a fool would listen to what he hadn't seen with his own eyes.

Still, Jeremy had studied the Book of the Prophets, and he knew full well that a wicked King could cause the whole earth to be cursed because of his evil. Jeremy was very anxious about any careless plot to get rid of the King, but he also wanted to know if the King really did need to be removed. If he did, then Jeremy himself was ready to help throw him down, much as the idea scared him.

So, on a time when Amagon had recently returned to the House from a journey, and there was little else to do, Jeremy went quietly to the master suite. He had seen no one in that part of the House as he came along the passage, but he spoke quietly nevertheless. It wouldn't do at all to be overheard. He began only by mentioning the wicked things he'd heard about the King, for he thought that would be the safest way to bring up the subject.

"Yes, everything you've heard about the King is true," Lord Amagon told him when Jeremy finished, his face setting into hard lines of disgust, "and it may be that soon we shall have to raise up a wiser man to take his place. But don't speak of these things, boy, for the walls have ears. . . even in Cerise. Yes, even in my own house there are spies, and Joseph would not hesitate to imprison or kill me, or you, or anyone else if even the whisper of such words ever reached his ears. Be careful what you say!"

Jeremy obediently nodded his head, but didn't fail to notice the comment about finding a wiser man to be King. He wondered exactly who Amagon meant by "we", and whether his secretive journeys and strange mood lately might possibly mean anything. He was almost afraid to ask, but he had to know.

"Sir, I have heard. . . tales, that some kind of plot to overthrow the King is already going on," he said. It wasn't exactly a question; he just wanted to see what Amagon would say. If he hadn't known the Master of the House better, he would have sworn he saw a glint of fear in Lord Amagon's eyes.

"Never say such a thing again, not even to me. You would have earned certain death for both of us with those words, if any spy had overheard you," Lord Amagon whispered.

"But sir, is it not very dangerous that such rumors are being passed along in the city, and that even I have heard them?" Jeremy persisted, also whispering.

"It's more dangerous than you can possibly imagine. Which is why I warn you to say nothing! Attract no suspicion! Don't admit you've even heard such things, and above all never repeat them to others. If you value your life, then hold your tongue!" Amagon said sharply.

Jeremy noticed that Lord Amagon hadn't exactly denied that a conspiracy was in the air. That alone was alarming. Amagon was normally one of the most open and truthful men Jeremy had ever known; not at all the kind of man who kept secrets without good reason. If he had believed the rumors were false then he would certainly have said so, or maybe told Jeremy not to repeat lies. Instead, he'd said nothing except to warn Jeremy to keep his mouth shut about anything he might hear. Therefore Jeremy felt certain something *was* going on, and that Lord Amagon was either involved with it in some way, or at least knew about it. That was exactly the sort of thing Jeremy had been dreading to hear, for whatever it was that the plotters might have had in mind, their scheme was already doomed. If Jeremy knew, then the King almost certainly also knew, and he would react with brutal force. Probably sooner rather than later. All this went through Jeremy's mind in only a few seconds. Then he immediately had to face the dangerous question of what he should do about it.

Lord Amagon was completely right about the danger of a careless tongue. Jeremy quickly decided that for now he would say nothing more about the subject. He also decided to keep an extremely close ear to the ground about what was being said in the city. He was afraid to be caught unprepared. There was one more thing he needed to say to the Master of the House, though.

"Sir, I fear the King has already heard the whispers in the city. Please, be careful," Jeremy asked earnestly. He could do nothing to help Lord Amagon except to plead caution. Whether or not it would do any good, he didn't know. Amagon only nodded without speaking, and so the interview ended.

Jeremy left the Master's suite and immediately went to his office above the pages' barracks. He locked the door behind him and began thinking hard about which boys he could trust. If a conspiracy was really afoot then Jeremy knew nothing about it for certain, but he also knew that even to be a trusted servant in the House of a man arrested for treason was very unsafe. Suspicion alone could mean a death sentence, as anyone who had dealt with King Joseph knew all too well. He would have to look into the matter at once, because it might well be that his own life was in danger, also.

Jeremy thought carefully. If the King's Guard came to arrest Amagon or anyone else in the House, they would likely do it late at night or just before dawn, so as to catch people asleep. Jeremy had more privacy than most others in the House, but everyone in the building knew where his rooms were located. He decided it would be unwise to spend any more time there.

The House was one of the largest in Cerise, and there were many parts of it which had lain empty for longer than anyone could remember. Several sections of the upper floors were not used, and so also was part of the south wing that butted up against the city wall. Any of these places might do very well as a hiding place in a pinch. Jeremy left his office and quietly climbed the back stairs to the fifth floor. He was very careful that no one should see him headed up there, for it was the kind of thing that might seem odd enough for someone to remember later on. At all costs, he mustn't do anything to attract attention.

It was silent as a cave in the upstairs hall. Jeremy could hear his own heart beating. The hall was long and wide, and rather dim. A little light came from a window at the very end of the passage, but only just enough to see his way. There was less dust than you might expect. Jeremy walked past door after door, all very much the same. He wanted to find a spare bedroom.

He reached for a door and opened the latch. Inside was a four poster bed bright with sunlight, and that wouldn't do. He needed a room with no window, for he dared not use a lamp in a windowed room. Someone outside might notice the light and come to investigate.

Such a room turned out to be difficult to find. Most of the rooms on the upper floors did have windows, and those which didn't were usually storage closets or other places unsuitable for sleeping. Jeremy did at last find a bedroom with no window; a small one at the back of the House, and if there had been a window there it would have looked out only at the stone wall of the city, ten feet away. This hadn't kept other rooms nearby from having windows (though covered with parchment instead of glass), and Jeremy could only guess that the room had been too small to deserve a window of its own.

However that might be, it suited Jeremy's purposes very nicely. He spent a good deal of the rest of the evening bringing up lamps, and extra oil, and food that wouldn't spoil, and some of his clothes, and a long rope, and things of that kind. He couldn't hurry, for he had to wait until he was certain no one was watching.

From then on he avoided his own rooms, and spent as little time in his office as possible. Jonah knew where he really was at all times, in case there should be an emergency he had to deal with right away, but Jonah could be trusted to tell no one else.

All this was done just in time. Two mornings later Jeremy awoke to find the household in an uproar, for soldiers had come in the early hours before dawn and taken Lord Amagon away, on a charge of plotting treason against the King.

The servants were trying to go about their work as if nothing had happened. Amagon didn't like disruption and chaos in his House no matter what the reason, and all knew it. Everyone was trying to live by his wishes. A casual visitor to the House would have noticed nothing unusual. But for anyone used to the daily atmosphere of the place, there was a subtle undercurrent of tension. No one was really paying proper attention to anything, so preoccupied were they with fear and uncertainty about the Master and what would become of the House (and of them).

Jeremy was in a better position to collect information than most of the others were, though. With a little thought, he was able to send boys on various errands to all of the great Houses in the city, and each of them reported directly to him anything they heard. He had no choice at this point but to choose the boys he considered most loyal, and pray that none of them were spies. He told them not to waste any time, and while they foraged for scraps of information, he quietly began to make preparations to flee the House, should it become necessary to depart immediately. He had no intention of allowing himself to be carried off to the King's dungeons. Very few ever came out again.

The distraction and general unease in the House helped him accomplish what he needed to do. People were too worried about themselves to pay much attention to anything he did. He was able to collect a good supply of ordinary clothes, dried food, some money, and other useful things, and hide them in a dark corner of the hay loft.

It was shortly before noon that his messengers began returning from all over Cerise, and very soon after that he heard the first rumor of his own arrest, from his friend Jonah, as it happened.

"Yes, sir, the captain of the guard said 'the boy with red hair in the house of Amagon', and there's no other such person in all of Cerise. They'll be here within an hour," the boy told him, breathless from running. Jeremy was alarmed, but he didn't lose his head. He'd half expected this very thing.

"Jonah, go quickly to the stable and saddle my pony, and be sure to pack the clothes and things you'll find in the northwest corner of the hay loft. Then come around to the back of the House as quickly as you can. At all costs I can't let them find me here," Jeremy ordered. He didn't wait to see if he were obeyed, for he knew Jonah was trustworthy. Jeremy left his office at once, hurrying back upstairs until he came to his hideout. He wasted little time there, just long enough to take the things he needed most. Then he went next door to one of the rooms with a window, and silently begged Amagon to forgive him before he tore the oilskin parchment off the window frame. No one must see him leaving the House. There were no exits except the front hall, the kitchen, and the stable, and there would be no way to avoid prying eyes if he went any of those places.

He stuck his head out the opening and looked down. It was at least forty or fifty feet to the ground, and Jeremy had to swallow a couple of times to gather his courage. A narrow alley ran between the back of the House and the city wall, with trash heaped up against both sides. After tossing out the sack of things he meant to bring, he tied his rope to one of the legs of the bed and pulled on it as hard as he could, to make sure it wouldn't give way. Then he put the other end out the window, and started to climb down. This didn't take much time, but the rope turned out not to be as strong as he thought. When he was still fifteen feet from the ground it snapped, sending him crashing to the ground. He landed on one of the piles of trash (he could hardly have avoided it), scattering rotten food and other nasty things everywhere. The trash broke his fall so it didn't hurt quite as much as it might have, but it knocked the breath out of him and twisted his elbow.

By the time he struggled to his feet, nursing his sore arm and brushing bits of garbage off his clothes, he saw Jonah coming up the alley, leading not just his own pony, but three others. There were two other boys behind him. Jeremy looked at him and raised his eyebrows.

"Why are Eli and Daniel with you?" he asked. It came out sounding nastier than he really meant it to, but he was desperate to get away from the House as fast as possible, and the unexpected change in plans put him out of temper.

"They already heard that you're to be arrested, sir, and they're not willing to let you flee into the wilderness alone. You wouldn't be able to survive. So, they brought their own ponies to go with you. . . and so have I," said Jonah. There was no time at all to argue about it just then, and Jeremy was touched that they cared so much as to put themselves in danger for his sake. He could only smile tiredly.

"Then come, my friends. I can never be grateful enough to repay your loyalty to me, so let's get out of the city before you suffer for it," he told them. With that there was no more talking.

## Chapter Six
### Flight

The four boys set out at once down the alley. Jeremy pulled his cap down low so no one could see his startling red hair, following Jonah's lead. He led them quickly into one of the slums on the east side of the city, and as soon as possible ducked into an empty warehouse. There was no telling how long the building had been abandoned. Judging by the holes in the roof and the rotten floor, it must have been a long time indeed. Hopefully, that meant nobody was likely to notice or care about their presence there.

Once inside, Jonah immediately began stripping off his diamond-encrusted livery and stuffing it into the saddle bags of his little pony. The others wasted no time doing the same. Jonah had brought some of the plain leather which the stable boys wore when they cleaned out the ponies' stalls, and they all dressed in this. It was at least clean, Jeremy thought, wrinkling his nose at the faint smell of horse manure that still reached his nose.

"I thought we might sell the livery in another town, to make up for the fact that we didn't have time to gather much food and supplies," Jonah said when they finished dressing.

Jeremy was impressed with such quick thinking. He felt strangely dependent on these other boys, and discovered he wasn't used to that. He'd become much too used to being in charge, he thought to himself. They all still expected him to lead them, but he knew he was going to have to lean heavily on their skills right now, just to survive the night.

"Boys, we need to find a way out of the city, as soon as we possibly can. The captain of the guard has probably already been to the House and found me gone. It might be a little longer before anybody notices you three missing too, but you can be sure it won't take longer than a few hours before somebody does. The King's Guard will hear about it, and they'll almost surely think you're with me. Then all our lives will be in danger. You may not have known what you were getting into at first, but I want to give you this one last chance to go back home," Jeremy told them.

None of the others said anything at first, and finally the silence became uncomfortable. Eli was the first one to break it.

"Sir, you found me starving on the streets when I had nothing. You gave me a place in the greatest House in the city, and all I have I owe to you. I refuse to abandon you now, just because the hour has become evil," he said. Jeremy turned a little red, but said nothing to this. Then Jonah spoke.

"Jeremy, for all these years I've been proud to call you my friend. When you were made pagemaster, I was glad because I knew you'd be a fair and kind leader. I haven't been wrong. You never forgot our friendship, and I won't forget it now. I won't leave you any sooner than Eli," he said.

"Nor I, sir," said Daniel, "I'm the newest of all the pages, and I don't know you well, but these are my friends, and it would be cowardly to run away from danger."

Jeremy didn't know what to say to all this praise, so he wisely said nothing at all. He could see there was no point in trying to convince the others to stay behind. The best thing he could do was accept their loyalty gracefully, and try to lead them as best he could. They were young, though. . . Jonah was sixteen, a year younger than Jeremy, but Eli was still only fifteen and Daniel not even that much. Jeremy didn't know him well enough to be sure of his age anymore.

"How old are you, Daniel?" he asked.

"Thirteen, sir," he replied promptly. Jeremy didn't like this, but decided he would be specially careful of Daniel. He was big for a thirteen-year-old. . . Jeremy could only hope he was wiser than his years, too.

"All right then, let's decide what to do. We need to leave the city at once, but that may not be easy. If we head for the gates I'll be recognized and most likely arrested. Even if we did get through, the guards would remember me. It would be much better to keep our departure a secret for as long as possible, because then the King's Guard will be hunting me inside the city, and may not think to look for us outside Cerise. At least not for a while. Do any of you have any ideas?" Jeremy asked.

"We could wait till after dark, then climb up on the walls and lower ourselves down by rope," Jonah suggested. Jeremy considered this.

"Too dangerous, I think. Someone might see us, even at night, and it would take a fool not to know something suspicious was going on. We'd have to leave the ponies behind, too. Worst of all, we'd have to wait inside the city all day. I'm afraid to give the Guard that many extra hours to look for us," Jeremy pointed out.

"If we need to get outside the walls without anybody seeing, then I might know a way," Eli told them, "Under the city, there's an aqueduct that flows down from the Blue River almost a mile upstream. It carries water to the main well in the central plaza, and to some of the wealthier houses and public pumps. It flows out of the city and back into the Blue River a little way downstream. Usually it would be impossible to enter it because of the force of the water, but since the river is so low. . . who can tell?"

"But we could never get our ponies down there, even if all four of us could somehow climb down the well," Jeremy objected.

"Let me finish, sir. There's a tunnel that slopes down to the aqueduct from near the Builders Hall, which is for the purpose of allowing access to the aqueduct whenever the walls need to be repaired. I found it long ago because it's one of the few places in the city which is never locked, and many of those with no other place to go take shelter there in the winter. No one will be there during the summertime, and it should be possible for us to escape without being noticed. I don't believe anyone would think to check that way," Eli said. Jeremy pondered this; he'd certainly never heard of the access tunnel before, and he doubted very much if the King's Guard would think to look there anytime soon, if they thought of it at all. It sounded promising.

"Let's go, then. Eli, you lead us," he decided.

The four boys led their ponies through the streets, trying not to attract attention. Jeremy couldn't go anywhere in Cerise without being instantly recognized, and that was the very last thing they wanted. He kept his cap pulled down low on his forehead and the collar of his jacket turned up, in spite of the summer heat. Sweat soon began to trickle down his back and his forehead, getting into his eyes and stinging. No doubt he smelled like a boar hog, he thought to himself. But if he did, Daniel and Jonah were pretending not to notice, and Eli was too far ahead to care. It was a considerable distance from the warehouse to the Builder's Hall. Eli avoided crowds whenever he could, choosing deserted alleys and little-used streets whenever possible. There were times when they had no choice but to cross a busy avenue, and they hurried through these places with hearts in their throats, expecting at any minute to feel the heavy hand of a guard from behind. But that didn't happen, and finally they came to the grounds of the Builders Hall. There they discovered a nasty surprise.

Eli led them directly to the tunnel mouth, which was, indeed, very rarely used to judge by its condition, but it was certainly being used now. A table had been set up to block access. Three men in the brown tunic of the Builder's Hall were sitting at the table. As the boys watched, they saw a young woman approach the table, hand the men several coins, and walk away with a pot of water. The men were selling water! For a moment, Jeremy was furious. They had to be stealing that water from the aqueduct, knowing full well how desperately low the supply was getting.

"What now? Those men will never let us into the tunnel," Jonah finally said.

Jeremy thought about it, and his anger slowly cooled into disgust. The men were no better than thieves, and it ought to be possible to bribe them without too much trouble. He reached into his saddle bag and carefully ripped loose four of the smaller diamonds from his livery, and showed them to the others.

"They'll let us through, in return for these. Four diamonds is more than they could earn in a whole month of selling water," he said.

"What if these scum have loose tongues? I don't doubt they would betray us to the Guard, if they thought any reward might be had," Eli said scornfully.

"I think that may be a chance we have to take," Jonah whispered. "We can't hide forever inside the city walls without being discovered, and if we don't soon find a way to escape, then we'll all be hung before the next sunset. The King takes no chances at all. Amagon may be able to count on a long prison sentence, because he's a wealthy and important noble. We're only four boys that no one will ever hear of again."

"Is there any other way into the tunnel?" Jeremy asked, without much hope.

"There might be a way down from inside the Builder's Hall, but getting in there would attract even more attention than bribing these three," Eli said. Jeremy sighed.

"Let's go, then," he said.

"Sir?" Daniel spoke up. Jeremy looked around at the youngest boy in the group and waited for him to speak.

"When Jonah and Eli were with me in the stable, I thought it might be a good idea to bring these along, since we didn't have any weapons," he said, reaching into his pack and pulling out four of the dart guns used by Amagon's riders. There were lions in the desolate lands between Cerise and the dye mines, and they were known to attack careless men and horses now and then. Those whose business took them to the mines or the northern farms always carried a gun for protection. They were powerful enough to stun a full grown lion within seconds. They had to be, for sometimes a couple of seconds was the only warning a man got. Jeremy had never seen one used before, but he knew there were times when they had saved a rider's life.

"Excellent, Daniel!" he cried. The others were no less delighted, and there was a great deal of back slapping and silent cheers. Daniel handed one of the guns to each of them, but by that time Jeremy had had time to think of a problem.

"Does anybody know how to use these weapons?" he asked. None of them did. For a minute there was a dreadful pause.

Jonah looked at his gun and finally smiled.

"You know, it really couldn't be that hard. They never let the stable boys handle these very much when I worked there, but I did see them used a time or two. It always looked like all you had to do was aim and pull the trigger. How hard could that be? What

I'm more interested in is how many darts they hold," he said.

They soon found that each gun held three darts. Daniel hadn't known where the extras were kept, but no one blamed him for that. They all agreed it ought to be easy enough to buy more of them, once they got away from Cerise.

Eli pointed his gun at the wall of a nearby building and pulled the trigger. There was barely a sound, and the dart was so small that at first they couldn't find it. But after some careful searching, they found the tiny sliver of wood embedded in one of the wall planks. Jeremy pulled it loose from the wood without too much trouble. It was barely as long as his little fingernail, and still wet with whatever drug the guns used. He wiped his fingers clean on the side of the building after handling the spent dart. He wasn't sure if the poison was strong enough to affect him just by touching it, but he didn't intend on taking any chances.

"This is the plan, then," he told the others, "What we'll do is wait until nobody else is close by, and then we'll go up to the table like we want to buy some water. That should keep all three of them busy at once. Whenever you get a chance, stun them. It's a crime to sell water that belongs to the city like that, so they won't dare report what happened."

"Just one thing, sir," Jonah said, "We all think you should stay here. You're too recognizable, and even if those men don't dare report us, we still don't want them to know who we are." Jeremy at once saw the sense in that, even though he didn't much like it.

"Go, then, and be quick!" he said.

Jonah, Eli, and Daniel left Jeremy in the alley and approached the table. Jeremy couldn't see what was happening very well at that distance, but in a few seconds he did see all three men drop like stones to the ground. He hurried up to the tunnel mouth to rejoin his friends. Eli was laughing.

"You should have seen the look on their faces! They didn't even have time to say a word before we dropped them like sheep. Come on," he urged the others, immediately heading into the tunnel.

"Wait!" Jeremy called to them.

"We can't just leave them like this. . . it might attract attention. If someone comes to buy water and finds them like that, the Guard might even hear about it. That's the last thing we want. We need to drag them a little way into the tunnel so no one will see them. They'll wake up in a few hours, but till then we want them out of sight. Jonah, I want you to take their moneybag. . . they earned that gold by cheating the people of the city, and I don't want them to profit by it. Then, too, I want them to think we were only robbers so maybe they won't suspect what our real reason was," he told them.

"Wouldn't that be stealing?" Jonah asked, uncertain. Jeremy wasn't completely sure about that himself, but he told them what he thought.

"This money didn't really belong to these thieves anyway, and we can't give it back to the people who really own it. If we just kept it and used it ourselves, then it might be stealing, but we aren't going to do that. Watch," Jeremy told them. He reached into his pocket and pulled out the four loose diamonds he'd torn off his livery.

"These diamonds are worth more than all the gold in this bag, and this is what I'm going to do. We're going to keep the gold coins, because they'll be easier to spend. But, I'm going to leave these diamonds here. This is a poor neighborhood, and whoever finds them, I wish him well." With that, Jeremy drew back his fist and threw the diamonds as far down the street as he could. They landed far away from the tunnel mouth, and Jeremy pronounced a blessing upon them, that they should be found by whoever needed them most. He turned to the others and smiled.

"There now! We can be sure we've done our part." The others accepted this and smiled also. They dragged the sleeping bodies of the Builder Hall men far enough into the tunnel mouth that no one could see them from the street outside, and then led their ponies deeper inside, following Eli once more.

It got cooler as they went down, and the stonework dripped with moisture. Slowly the bright tunnel mouth shrank to a pinprick behind them, then vanished completely around a curve. No one had thought to bring a lantern, and they were forced to walk in total darkness. None of them liked this at all, and at Eli's suggestion they took a coil of rope and tied themselves together, so they wouldn't get separated in the dark.

There was no sound except the drip, drip, drip of the wet walls, until with a cry of surprise Eli splashed into water. He stumbled and fell, soaking himself from head to toe, but he soon regained his footing, since the water was not, after all, very deep.

"Come on," he called to the others, who were waiting at the lip of the tunnel. His voice echoed weirdly in the enclosed space.

"We made it to the aqueduct, and the water is no more than two feet deep. The bottom is all gravel and stone, so don't worry about your footing," he added. The others gingerly waded out into the underground river, and moved slowly downstream. Jeremy thought it might be a good idea to keep track of how far they walked, and began counting his footsteps.

None of them said much during that long, cold, disagreeable journey. The tunnel was perfectly round, though it was hard to tell exactly how big around it might be. The bottom was layered with a thin bit of sand and gravel, which made footing a little bit better than if it had been plain stone. The water never got deeper than knee-height, and sometimes fell to no more than ankle depth. Jeremy had counted almost five thousand steps when they began to see the first glimmers of light ahead. Almost two miles. The light grew steadily brighter, until they stood blinking at the lip of a stone tube, from which a calf-high stream of water poured forth as a waterfall to rejoin what was left of the Blue River.

They could see the tunnel mouth was usually located far below the water line of the river. No one would ever find it unless he knew exactly where to look. The people of Cerise were careful about enemies.

They left the tunnel mouth, having to brace themselves against the current to keep from being knocked off their feet. The ponies gave them a hard time, and could only be forced to jump down when

Jonah climbed back inside the tunnel and gave them a sharp sting with his whip. They all splashed across the shallow river and clambered up the bank as best they could. It was a ticklish task, but presently all four of them stood on the east bank of the Blue River with their ponies, none the worse for wear except for a little wetting.

## Chapter Seven
## The High Plain

Cerise lay almost a mile upstream, and all that could be seen of it through the woods were the upper turrets and a few of the towers of the greater houses. The South Road which led to Rustrum hugged the west bank of the river, never more than a stone's throw from the water. It suited Jeremy just fine for the road to be on the far bank, for there might be soldiers passing back and forth along that way, and they had no wish to meet any emissaries of the King.

They melted into the edge of the woods, far enough from the river bank that they couldn't be seen, and there they held a council of war.

"What are our choices, Jonah?" Jeremy asked. Jonah knew more about the countryside than any of the others, for he liked geography.

"None of the choices are very good ones, I'm afraid. If we keep going south, we'll soon run out of water. Not many miles downstream the river sinks into the dust. The empty riverbed keeps going on for almost a hundred miles until it comes to Rustrum, but none of those lands would be safe. Soldiers pass that way constantly. If by chance we did make it through, I don't see how it would help us to run right into the lion's den. There are more spies in Rustrum than there are here."

"To the west is the land of the Sohrab. They would enslave us or turn us over to the King without a second thought, if we encountered them."

"If we go north, we'd run into the garrison of soldiers who guard the dye mines, but even if we got past them it wouldn't do us any good. Beyond the mines are the Cesmean Mountains, full of the Lachishite barbarians who despise the Most High. Those people are drinkers of blood and killers of children, and only the King's army protects Cerise from them,"

"And the east?" Jeremy asked grimly.

"Just the High Plain. Dead, empty county for the most part. That was the first place the drought destroyed. But if you go on, then far across the empty lands you'd come to the Eyre Hills and the upper valley of the Murray. There might still be some life in that region, but I couldn't say for sure," Jonah finished. The boys digested this for a few moments.

"The Sohrab took me from a village in the Eyre Hills," Jeremy said quietly. "I don't know what kind of reception I'd get after all this time, and I don't know what the four of us would do there even if they welcomed us. They're simple folk who raise cows, mostly. Not much use there for reading or high courtesy or swordplay. But maybe. . . " Jeremy trailed off, deep in thought. Going home gave him all sorts of mixed feelings, and he really wasn't sure yet what he thought about that idea. The others kept quiet and let him think.

"The High Plain sounds like our best bet, for now. I don't think anyone will look for us there," he finally said.

"If we want to get up onto the Plain, then we'll have to take the old east road from Cerise. It's the only way. The edge of the Plain is sheer, and thousands of feet high, all the way south to Rustrum," Jonah told them.

Jeremy nodded, encouraging him to go on.

"Once we reach the top of the Plain, the old road will finally take us to a place named Thaloth. That's a dead city about forty miles from the cliff's edge, or maybe sixty miles from Cerise. There *might* still be water there, or at least enough for the four of us and our ponies. I've never been that far, myself," Jonah admitted.

"And if there isn't?" Eli asked.

"Thaloth is the biggest city on the Plain, and it probably has the deepest well. If it's dry, then we'll have to either come back down here or else try to go on and reach the Hills," Jonah said, shrugging as if it didn't make much difference to him either way. Jeremy knew he was pretending not to care as a way to cover up his fear. He couldn't read the others well enough to know what they were thinking, but Jonah was an open book. He guessed they were just as scared as Jonah was.

Jeremy couldn't let them sit still much longer, in that condition. If they had time to think too much, they might do something stupid like try to return to Cerise. It was much too late for that now, for any of them.

"Let's get going, then," he said briskly, standing up and heading for his pony. His firmness got them moving again, which he knew was the very thing they needed most.

Jonah led them again now. They were about two miles from the east road, but he didn't want to reach the road too close to Cerise. What little traffic there was, farmers or woodcutters, was likely to be near the city. They much preferred that no one at all should see them. For that reason he meant to cut through the forest at a slant, and come to the road a few miles east of Cerise, where it was likely to be deserted.

This they did, and had no problems finding the road. The forest was thin and had little undergrowth, for the people of Cerise often came there to collect fallen limbs for firewood, which kept the forest clear. They stepped out onto the dusty highway after about two hours of walking, and found it, as they expected, deserted. The road had begun to sprout bits of grass and bracken here and there, though the lack of rain had kept the green things from attacking the highway as much as they might have done.

They made haste to ride eastward as quickly as they could go. The somber cliffs of the Plain loomed up before them, not quite fifteen miles away, and they knew they would have to reach the top before resting. It wouldn't be safe to pitch camp so close to Cerise.

So they rode on, and both they and the ponies were very tired indeed before the task was done. They reached the base of the cliffs just as the moon rose, casting a deep pool of black shadow all around them. The east road climbed up onto the Plain through a straight cutting, with a steep, steady slope that the boys soon began to feel they would never be able to finish. At one time there had been rest stations in little buildings along the way, where a traveler could refresh himself with water and a comfortable spot to sit down for a few minutes. Only the buildings and the couches were still there. Each of the boys had a full waterskin, from which he drank as sparingly as he could. There was no chance of refilling them before Thaloth, and that was still two days journey away.

At last they reached the top of the cliff, exhausted by the long climb. They were met by a cold breeze blowing from the east, and the sight of the High Plain unfolding before them into the silver distance beneath the moon. Jeremy turned back to the west and stood in awe at the view. All the valley of the Blue lay spread out below him, and beyond that the lowlands stretched far into Sohrabia. Cerise was a tiny city built of blocks. Far, far to the south, so that he couldn't be quite sure he saw it, Jeremy noticed a silver glint that might have been the sea. The edge of the Plain at this point dropped almost five thousand feet to the river valley below him, and he was very glad indeed that they wouldn't have to climb it again.

They decided it was worthwhile to go on a little farther that night, in the hope of coming to a deserted farm where they would have shelter. It was cold on the High Plain at night, even in the summer. There was already a shiver in the air as they came up out of the cutting, and they soon had to stop and unpack some of the warmer things in their saddlebags. That took a certain amount of doing, because everything had been thrown together hastily when they fled the city. Clothes were jumbled up with food and tools and everything else. But it was done at last, and they went on.

After a while, they grew tired of talking. The cold air made their mouths dry and left an unpleasant dusty taste on their tongues. For a while they looked around them at the passing countryside. The moon lit up the gray and silver landscape with a ghostly glow, showing many farms and orchards dotted across the rolling plateau. The High Plain had been a pretty sort of place, before the drought came.

The boys didn't have to ride very far before they found a little house set amidst a grove of dead and withered peach trees. By then the night had grown shockingly cold, and all four of them halted in front of the farmstead without even any need to discuss the matter. It was built of whitewashed slate, like most of the houses they had seen, and turned out to contain just two rooms. One of the rooms had a stone fireplace which seemed to still be in working order.

Jonah saw to settling the ponies in for the night while the other three ventured back outside with hatchets to cut and split some wood for a fire. They soon found that dead wood is hard to chop, and Jeremy wished more than once for a proper axe, instead of a little hatchet. It didn't take long before they gave up on cutting down a whole tree. There were a few pieces of wood already lying scattered on the ground, and they discovered it was possible to hack off some of the smaller branches without too much difficulty. They stacked a large pile of this inside the house, but not too near the hearth, lest it catch fire during the night.

There was soon a bright fire of peach wood burning in the old grate. The stone walls held the warmth, and the boys were soon quite snug. There were two beds in the other room, with straw tick mattresses. They dragged these into the living room near the fire. Jeremy shared a mattress with Eli, lying back to back and covering themselves with both their blankets to stay warm. Jonah and Daniel did the same on the other mattress.

The other three fell asleep right away, but Jeremy found himself too full of thoughts. Now that he had time to think, without the constant need to simply survive from minute to minute, he was beginning to wonder what he planned to do with himself, and where he would lead these boys who had staked their lives to follow him. Getting to Thaloth was one thing, and it was a workable goal for the moment. They might even find enough food and water there to stay in the old city for a long time, but then what? Jeremy didn't find the idea of hiding out in a dead city for the rest of his life very appealing, and he didn't think the others would like it any better. He didn't relish the idea of crossing the whole Plain and going up into the Eyre Hills, either. The best they could hope for in that region was a life of cow herding, and in the end that really wasn't much different than hiding in Thaloth. There had to be a better plan, if he could only think of one.

Jeremy shivered a little as the fire began to die down, pulling the blankets closer around him. He was too tired to think and too anxious not to.

He spent a moment in prayer about it, committing himself and all of them to the care of the

Most High, and afterwards he felt reassured, as he always had.

Jeremy had no doubt that things would work out as they should, for he had studied the Book of the Prophets for a long time. The first verse he had ever learned, long ago, was that the Most High would never forsake those who trusted Him.

He remembered, a little wistfully, that he'd been a very little boy when he learned that verse. . . no more than five or six years old, on a gray afternoon in midwinter, when it was too cold to play outside. On days like that, the priest would sometimes gather up the village children and teach them things. Letters and numbers, old songs, verses from the Book of the Prophets, or tales of the wide world. The priest was very old, but he had a good voice for things like that. Jeremy hadn't thought about him in years, and now, on the drowsy edge of sleep in a cold and forsaken place, he could almost hear the words of the priest as he read the verses.

Although Jeremy didn't know it, the priest had noticed his quick mind and his interest in the lessons, and had taken it upon himself to ensure that the strange red-haired boy was given more time and attention than any of his other students. This was partly the reason for Melech's jealousy, and for his parents' coolness, for they all knew that this boy was not meant for the herder's life. For his parents, that had meant that sooner or later they would have to let him leave the village. It was likely they'd never see him again after that, and so they had made an effort for a long time not to become too attached to what they must certainly lose. Melech was the one they loved best, for they knew (and Melech knew), that he would never be more than a shepherd of cows.

Jeremy knew none of these things, of course, and wouldn't have believed it even if anyone had told him. All he knew was that the distant memory of learning the Book was a comfort to him now, when he had most reason to be afraid. He fell asleep with that thought in his mind.

### *Chapter Eight*
### *Prophet*

The next morning dawned cool and breezy, as most days did on the High Plain. The boys found their fire burned to ashes in the grate, and the room was chilled. Eli went to the saddlebags to fetch something for breakfast while the others explored the house a little more thoroughly. Jonah found several extra blankets on an upper shelf, and they gladly wrapped themselves in these. There was a well behind the house which turned out to be dry as dust. It gave them all the most gloomy thoughts about what might be waiting for them at Thaloth, but none of them wanted to say so.

They ate a very meager breakfast of dried meat jerky, and packed up quickly. The sun had just risen above the edge of the Plain, a red ball of molten gold. All was silent as only the very early morning can be. No birds sang. For a while they wrapped in blankets to keep off the chill, but soon the sun warmed the air to the point that they didn't need them anymore.

They traveled that day through what seemed like endless miles of withered orchards and farmland, now and then passing through little villages built of gray and white stone. Each of these places had a well in the village square, and they checked all of them for water, just in case. All were empty. The High Plain had been dead for a long time.

Jeremy could almost imagine he recognized occasional places and things as they went along. An oddly shaped tree beside the ditch, or a particularly big house. They teased his memory. He guessed the Sohrab caravan that brought him to Cerise must surely have used that same road, all those years ago, but one part of the Plain looked so much like any other part, he could never be quite sure.

A little before noon they stopped in one of the larger villages to eat a bit and drink some water. They had expected it would become hot as the day went on, but that turned out not to be the case. The high country was quite comfortable, except that the sun was fiercely bright that day, glaring off the pale ground and hurting their eyes. They all pulled their caps down lower to shut out the light as much as possible.

They saw no one all day, and spent a second night in an empty farmstead. This one wasn't nearly as comfortable as the first one. It had no mattresses they could use, and they discovered (too late) that the top of the chimney had collapsed and blocked the opening. That meant no fire. There were also cracks in the wall where the wind blew whistling through all night long, slipping its cold fingers into every blanket and cloak. None of them slept very well.

They woke very early the next morning, still tired after a sleepless night. Jeremy thought about going on just as far as the next usable house and then resting all day, but a look at his near-empty waterskin soon convinced him otherwise.

They came to the outer walls of Thaloth just as the sun sank slowly behind the western rim of the Plain. The old iron gates stood open, and the boys passed inside without saying much, too tired to be excited. They headed immediately for the central square, to see if the main well still had water or not. Their waterskins were almost empty. If they found the well dry, they would have to make some serious decisions at once. They could either head back to Cerise, or try to make a desperate forced march to cross the rest of the Plain and reach the Murray river as it came down out of the hills. Both choices would be dangerous.

In spite of such gloomy thoughts, they couldn't help noticing that Thaloth was a rather nice city. The avenues were broad and straight, radiating from the center like spokes on a wheel. The buildings were carved with pictures of animals and humans, with exquisite attention to detail. Most of it was built of a silvery-white stone, sometimes painted, sometimes not.

Jonah told them various things about the city as they rode along, to pass the time. It had once been the largest city on the High Plain and the seat of the governor, and a place which had always been considered specially holy to the Most High. The others listened to all this with half an ear, only mildly interested. Jonah had always liked knowing things like that.

Everything they saw gave the impression of people who had enjoyed life and been happy in their high city. Jeremy wondered where all of them had gone. Probably not many people had actually starved to death when the drought came. Most of them must simply have gone elsewhere. He could imagine them streaming down into the valley of the Blue or the Murray, and rebuilding their farms in the still-fertile lowlands. Some of them might even still live in Cerise, and that made him curious if he'd ever known any of them. Who could tell?

Occupied with these thoughts, Jeremy almost didn't notice when they emerged into the central plaza. There was indeed a well there, very deep, and it took a long time to lower the bucket all the way down on its rusty chain. This time they were rewarded with a faint splash almost beyond hearing. Daniel smiled and began to draw the water up from deep inside the earth.

Soon the ponies were drinking thirstily at the troughs nearby, and all the skins were refilled. Jeremy felt much better about things now. With water, they could survive in Thaloth a long time, and that would give him a while to think of what to do next.

The old palace of the Governor of the High Plain faced the square from the west, and the boys decided to set up living quarters in that building while they remained in the city. They explored it a little bit with lanterns, not liking to sleep in a place so full of shadowy corners and dark rooms. The silence and the emptiness made them ill at ease. They spoke in whispers and tip-toed through the cavernous halls, as if someone might hear them. No one wanted to mention ghosts, but it was the kind of place that made you think about them whether you wanted to or not.

They found bedrooms and feasting halls and armories full of swords and axes. There were still tapestries on the walls and even tablecloths in the dining room. A thick layer of dust had settled on everything, with not a single footprint except their own. After looking at several of the rooms, they gave up the expedition. It would have taken days and days to see the whole palace. None of them really wanted to explore too much of that cold, dead place by night. Much better to wait for the sun.

In the meantime, they claimed the guardhouse for their own. It was only a single room, not too large, and it suited their purposes very well.

Over the next few days they did explore the palace (which looked amazingly ordinary in daylight), and much of the rest of the city and the lands nearby.

One thing they didn't find was any food. Jeremy started to worry about that until Jonah reminded him they would have to find the city granary where all the corn and wheat would have been kept safe from pests. Anything edible that might have been left behind in the palace or elsewhere would have long since been eaten by rats. The granary itself probably didn't contain more than a little corn, but what there was ought to still be good. The dry air would have kept it from rotting, even after many years. So they hoped, at least.

None of them knew how to do much with dry corn. Jeremy guessed they could probably grind it up in a pestle and make some kind of mush out of it, or maybe bread if they could figure out how to bake it.

"Bread and water," Eli grumbled, with a disgusted look on his face.

"Stop whining, Eli. . . what if we had no food at all?" Jonah scolded him. Eli subsided, but he still didn't look happy.

They knew it was unlikely anyone would come looking for them, but they still didn't want to advertise their presence in the city any more than necessary. One could never be completely certain who might pass that way. Sohrab caravans crossed the Plain once in a while, and there were criminals and outlaws in the wild lands, too. It wasn't impossible that any of these people might visit the city at times, for water or shelter or other reasons. Therefore the boys went quietly through the city, not singing or talking too loud, and they never went alone.

The main reason for these expeditions was to look for the granary. They were also a good way to pass the time, though. Besides exploring, there wasn't much else to do in Thaloth. Jeremy had never imagined how boring a city could be, with no people in it.

It was on one of these trips through the city that Jeremy found the direction he'd been looking and praying for ever since they first fled Cerise.

He was with Jonah that time, talking about nothing in particular. They were riding down a dusty street somewhere on the north side of the city, when they passed a building unlike anything they had yet seen. It was taller than most, built of the same silver-white stone as the rest of the city. What made it remarkable was the color. It had been painted with the blue dye of Cerise. Jeremy couldn't imagine how much money it must have cost to color an entire building blue. Both of them stood there in awe.

"Should we go find Daniel and Eli?" Jonah asked in a hushed voice.

"Let's see what's inside first; it might not be anything much," Jeremy said. They got down off their ponies and went to look at the building more closely.

It had wide front doors like the entrance to a church, and four huge pillars on the front which supported a kind of porch with steps that led up to the doors. When they came to the top of the seventh step, the boys found the big doors locked, as they had halfway expected. There was a keyhole which could have swallowed an entire hand, but whoever had been in charge of the building was long gone, and the keys with him. Jonah rattled the latch, but it was firmly shut.

"There has to be a way in," he said, looking around the porch as if he expected to find the key lying somewhere by his feet.

"Maybe," Jeremy said absently, running his fingers across the golden latch.

"I think-" Jonah began.

"I still have the keys to Lord Amagon's house," Jeremy mentioned, without much hope. It was the only thing he could think of. He felt a little guilty for running off with Master Amagon's keys. He was the only other person besides Amagon himself who was entrusted with a copy of the key to the front doors of the House, since there was no telling when or for how long the Master might be away from home these past few months. Amagon's copy was no doubt locked up in prison with him, and the other servants of the House were probably finding it difficult to lock the doors at night. Jeremy hoped nobody had tried to break in, but then he dismissed that thought. There was nothing he could do about it now.

"Go ahead and try them, I guess," Jonah said, looking skeptical. Jeremy pulled out his key ring and brought it up to the door, and quickly saw that all the keys were too small, except possibly the key to Lord Amagon's front doors. Jeremy took that one and inserted it into the keyhole, and to his surprise the key turned. He looked at Jonah before taking his key back and putting it in his pocket.

"Now who would have thought we'd be so lucky as that?" he said. He thought nothing more of it, yet.

"With you, nothing is ever luck," Jonah replied cryptically, with a mysterious smile on his face. It was a strange remark, and Jeremy glanced at him with furrowed brows for a second, wondering what it was supposed to mean. Jonah didn't seem disposed to clarify things, so Jeremy finally shrugged and let it go. There were more important things to think about.

He reached up and grasped the latch. The door swung outward slowly on silent hinges, bringing with it the stale odor of dry air that has stood still too long. It wasn't quite dark inside, for there were small windows high up on the walls, cleverly hidden so they weren't visible from outside. There was also a thick layer of dust on the floor, as if the building hadn't been opened for a very long time. That was all they could see from the outside.

Jeremy took a step forward into the building, and Jonah followed, kicking up a cloud of dust that made them want to sneeze. It was much easier to see in the dim light once they moved indoors. They saw now that the building was utterly empty, except for a short column of stone about four feet high in the exact middle, with some small thing that glittered gold sitting on top of it. Jeremy strode forward to examine the object more closely. Jonah followed more slowly, trying not to stir up the dust.

"There's an inscription on here!" Jeremy called back to Jonah, fully interested now. He peered at the small letters, trying to read them in the dim light. The stone seemed to be blue malachite or maybe some other kind of material he didn't recognize, and the dark color made it hard to read the letters. It took him some time to piece together all the writing, therefore, but after some effort this is what he read:

*Welcome, o long awaited Prophet!*
*And be glad, o longed-for King!*
*The land shall laugh with the falling rain,*
*And the righteous no more be ashamed.*
*Oh, taste and see, ye chosen one,*
*And take up the power of the Lord.*

Jeremy fell back in shock, sure they had intruded on a holy place not meant for them. Jonah had come up behind him while he was standing by the column, and was reading over his shoulder. He pulled at Jonah's arm as he headed hastily for the door.

"Where are you going?" the other boy asked him, not seeming the least bit rattled by the inscription.

"We have to get out of this place!" Jeremy hissed, pulling at his arm again. But Jonah resisted.

"Don't you see this message was left for you?" Jonah said calmly. At that idea Jeremy was even more afraid. . . whether because it might be true or because it might not be, he hadn't the faintest idea. He couldn't decide whether the feeling that welled up in his heart was wild hope or abject terror. . . or maybe both.

"Don't talk like that, Jonah; now be quiet and let's get out of here! Please!" Jeremy pleaded. Jonah shrugged a little bit and walked slowly to the door behind Jeremy, who had bolted from the room as if it contained a thousand poisonous snakes. He was trembling and couldn't speak when Jonah approached him.

"It has to be you, Jeremy," Jonah said firmly. "No one else would have had a key to that door today."

"Lord Amagon has a key," Jeremy protested, still not wanting to believe, "It must be talking about him!"

Jonah shook his head mildly, but with no doubt involved.

"Lord Amagon wasn't here today. You were. Do you believe the Most High leaves such things to chance?" Jonah demanded, "No, Jeremy; you know better than that. You've been chosen as a prophet, and that's a high and holy calling. Now get back in there and find out what you're supposed to do!"

Jeremy looked at him with eyes that showed his doubt, but Jonah wasn't disappointed in the boy he already admired more than anyone else in the world. Jeremy took a deep breath to calm himself, and then walked slowly back into the temple. He would pray, and perhaps the Most High would tell him what to do. Jonah shut the doors behind him, for who was he to intrude upon the prophet of the Most High? He stood guard outside, patiently waiting for Jeremy to emerge.

After an hour or so Jeremy did come out, looking very tired and dusty, and seemingly not much more at peace with his role than he'd been to begin with. Jonah noticed that he wore a golden amulet upon a chain around his neck.

"I don't know what this is for," he said quietly, pointing toward the necklace, "but I'm supposed to wear it all the time.  It was sitting on top of the pillar where the inscription was.  I won't say any more till we all four are together again."

Jonah accepted this agreeably, and together the two of them rode off toward the palace.  It was almost nightfall, and Daniel and Eli would be arriving soon. Jeremy didn't look forward to that.

When the two younger boys arrived at the palace, it was Jonah who told them eagerly about the great blue building, and the inscription, and the command of the Most High.  In the meantime Jeremy sat quiet and withdrawn in the corner, making no comment.  Daniel and Eli were electrified by the news, and when the story was over they sat looking at Jeremy with shining and worshipful eyes.  He hated it.

"This is the word of the Most High.  He is angry with the wickedness of the King of Rustrum, for his unrighteousness has reached even unto Heaven. That is why the drought has come to destroy the land, for the earth itself cannot abide his evil, and the people have followed their King.  To me has been given power over the clouds of the air, to make rain or not, until the King of Rustrum is destroyed, and all his works, and the people have returned to the righteousness of their youth.    We will go to Rustrum and demand the repentance of the people.  I have spoken," Jeremy said, in a voice of more authority and power than he would have believed possible.  When he was finished, the other boys were nodding solemnly, as if that were exactly what they had expected.

"My friends," he began in his own voice, "I'm glad you three are with me in this, because I don't know if I could face it all alone."  The others nodded as if they understood.  They didn't, of course, and never would, but Jeremy was content.

### *Chapter Nine*
### *War*

The next morning, rain fell on the High Plain for the first time in thirty years, a long, soaking rain of the kind that would sink deep into the parched earth. None of the boys had seen rain before, and couldn't get enough of looking at it, and walking in it, and talking about it. They didn't travel in it, but the thunder and wind that came with it were wonderful things just to bask in for a while.

Within a week, the High Plain had turned green with new shoots of grass, and the dark fields were full of sprouting bits of barley seed that had lain undisturbed for decades. The brooks and rills roared with unaccustomed flow, chattering toward the valley of the Murray far away. None of the water would ever reach that far, of course, and none but the occasional Sohrab trader would even notice what had been done on the High Plain, but the land would not soon forget.

The next day the boys rode south with a purpose, passing quickly through Beloth and Techirath, and several smaller cities on the road. Jonah didn't know the names of any others. It was almost a hundred miles from Thaloth to the southeastern edge of the Plain, where they hoped to strike the valley of the Murray. The well in Techirath still contained some water, and they gladly refilled their bottles there. It was never a bad idea to carry extra. A shower bath in the rain was a fine thing, but it was hard to satisfy thirst by standing still and waiting for drops to fall on one's tongue. The parched ground sucked up any moisture that fell on it almost instantly, leaving no puddles.

After about a week of steady riding they drew near to the valley of the Murray. The river itself was nothing but a wide ditch of gravel and dust, as they had expected. There was a small trickle of water in the very bottom, hardly noticeable among the shale and scree. Not far to the east Jeremy could glimpse the gentle folds of the Eyre Hills where he had been born.

He stood for a little while and wondered wistfully what had ever become of Melech and the rest of his family. Most likely they were still there, herding cows as they had always done. It might be that Melech was married by now, and living in his own house. Probably he was. He was old enough that Papa and Mama would have arranged something like that for him. Jeremy found the idea of anybody living with Melech hard to imagine, but he sighed and turned away.

At that point the road veered south to follow the riverbank, and the hills went out of sight behind them. Jeremy thought it was just as well, for he didn't want to be thinking of his family right then. He still had a mission to carry out.

It was no more than five miles before they came suddenly to the end of the road. The Murray plunged down from the High Plain in a fall of almost four thousand feet, or at least it would have, had there been any water to fall. The road went on as barely more than a footpath, looping back and forth down the face of the cliff until it reached the lowlands. It had been cut by hand out of the solid rock, at great cost, and it was a narrow and breathless way to take, with no rail to keep a traveller from plunging to his death if he made a careless step or if the wind gusted too hard. More than one of the boys shivered as he looked down the face of that horrible drop. They decided it would be far safer to walk down and lead the ponies, than it would be to try to ride them.

"Well, let's get going, boys," Jeremy said, trying to sound cheerful about it. The others took a little longer to gather their courage. Jeremy led the way, with his heart in his mouth as he stepped down onto the trail. It felt almost exactly like walking right off the edge of the cliff.

Then he met an obstacle. His pony came up to the very edge of the precipice, and there dug in her heels and refused to go any farther. Jeremy scrambled back up onto the cliff top with the others, secretly relieved to be on more solid ground again.

"What's wrong with her, Jonah?" he asked. Jonah looked glum.

"She doesn't like that narrow trail, and I can't say I blame her. She's not a goat. Neither am I, for that matter," Jonah said. Jeremy and the others laughed a little, but it was a nervous laugh of the kind that isn't really funny.

"Yes, but this is the only way down, isn't it?" Jeremy asked.

"As far as I've ever known or heard of, yes," Jonah shrugged.

"Except for the road from Cerise, that is," he added.

"That's no good. We can't go all the way back there. We don't have enough food, and it would waste weeks worth of time. We could be down in the valley before nightfall, if we go this way," Jeremy said.

"Yes, but not if the animals won't cooperate," Jonah pointed out. The other two had said nothing up till this point, but now Eli spoke up.

"Do we really need the ponies anyway? We can carry enough food and water and things for a day or two on our backs, and once we get down into the valley there will be people and villages where we can get more. Can't we just leave the ponies here and go on ourselves?" he asked. The others thought about that for a minute.

"But what would happen to them, if we leave them here?" Daniel objected. Eli looked a little uncomfortable about that himself, but didn't know what to say.

"The hills are close by, and there's still green things there. You can see it even from here. And the river still has a little water in it for them. I don't think anything lives up here anymore that would hurt them," Jeremy said.

"So you think we should leave them, and go on anyway?" Jonah asked.

"Yes. I don't see any other choice, Jonah. I grudge every minute the King is still in power to go on with his wickedness," Jeremy said firmly.

"All right, then," Jonah said. He began opening his saddlebags and taking out all the things packed inside. They would have to leave quite a lot of things behind, for a boy can't carry nearly so much as a horse.

As it turned out, they had to leave almost everything. They each took a large waterskin, enough food for about three days, and not much else. Each of them had a little bag of diamonds torn loose from the livery he had worn in Cerise, but the livery itself had to be abandoned. Also left behind were most of the warmer and thicker clothes they had brought. Tinderboxes they kept, and knives, and a few other items. Anything not strictly necessary they hid behind a large boulder near the road, just in case they should ever come back for any of it.

When all the sorting and repacking was done, they unsaddled the ponies and removed their bridles, and set them free with such blessing as they could give them. They hid the saddles and things with the other items behind the boulder, and prepared to tackle the cliff.

Jeremy went first, then Jonah, then Daniel, and finally Eli. The path was no more than four feet wide, and the cliff bulged out above them so they seemed to be walking inside a giant crack in the cliffside. At no point was it possible to get far enough from the edge not to be able to see how very high up they were. They hated to keep their eyes open and didn't dare close them. The wind scared them, for it was strong and gusty at times, so that if you were careless it might even sweep you off balance. One strong blast from behind did knock Eli off his feet, and if Daniel hadn't been close by to catch his arm, he would have rolled right off the edge of the cliff. He stood up pale and shaking, and it was a long time before the others trusted him to go on.

From time to time they came to a switchback, where the road bent back upon itself before continuing downward. In these spots there was a deeper cutout in the rock, and they had a little breathing space to rest.

All told, it took about seven hours to reach the bottom of the cliff. When at last they reached the flat ground and stood beside the wide and empty pool at the foot of the falls, Eli fell to the earth like a dead thing and kissed it three times before getting back up. No one laughed.

There was an empty village beside the pool, and from that point the road opened out again and ran on straight and sure, bound directly for Rustrum. They spent the night in the empty village, and early the next morning set out walking.

As they got closer to Rustrum, they found some of the villages along the riverbank still occupied. In each of these places Jeremy went directly to the town center and began to preach, demanding repentance from evil, and calling for the overthrow of the wicked King of Rustrum. At first people laughed, or didn't listen at all, but when he raised his hands to the empty sky and brought the rain pouring down, then no one laughed anymore. Everything was dropped so that people could hear him, and his words filled them with shame. Many repented of the wickedness they had committed, but those who didn't repent became only the angrier. King Joseph's spies didn't fail to report this story to the King at once, and he was filled with fury that anyone should dare to openly call for his downfall. He sent loyal members of his Guard to arrest all four boys immediately, but Jeremy never stayed in one place long enough to be trapped.

He soon reappeared, however, a little closer to Rustrum each time, and the tale of his doings followed him like wildfire. The people were eager to hear what he would say, for there had been no prophet in the land since the days of King Joseph's grandfather. Jeremy preached, and brought down rain upon the parched and dying land, and wherever he went, by the power of his words and the life-giving water at his command, the people were set free of the King. Soon, he marched at the head of an army of five thousand men from the freed villages, headed sternly toward Rustrum.

Now King Joseph was not by any means a coward, nor did he have any intention of giving up his throne to a red-haired boy who had come out of nowhere and commanded the rain. The King would have liked nothing better than to send an army to crush and kill the upstart, but he soon found that even his soldiers held the prophet in awe, and he dared not trust his own servants any longer.

Whatever villages repented of the wickedness of their fathers and returned to the path of righteousness received rain in abundance, while those who hardened their hearts and remained loyal to the King lay parched and dying beneath the blazing sun. Therefore the King determined to pretend to give up the fight, and to lure Jeremy to his palace in Rustrum, alone if possible, and then to kill the boy with his own hands. When the rebels saw the body of their great leader, dead at the hands of the King, they would be filled with even greater fear than ever before.  Indeed, it might yet turn out that the entire episode only hardened and solidified his power over Rustrum and all the land besides.  And the King laughed in the wickedness of his heart, for he had forgotten the Most High.

Thus it was that the King recalled his soldiers, and a new message was sent out, begging for pardon and a chance to speak with the prophet.  The messengers reached him in the town of Xanthus, on the bank of the Murray, about twenty miles north of Rustrum.  The people there had given Jeremy the largest house in the town, refusing to lodge him in any lesser place.  The King's messenger was deeply polite and even worshipful, but Jeremy gave him no answer at that time.  He wanted to talk with his friends first and consider what the King's intentions might be, under their fair cloak.  He hadn't by any means forgotten the King's reputation.

Jonah was suspicious at once.

"The King hasn't repented.  If he had, he would have come here himself and not sent a messenger.  He still has some plan to twist things for his own benefit-wait and see!"  he insisted.  Jeremy thought about this, but said nothing just yet.

"What do you others think?"  he asked quietly.

"I think Jonah is right. . . the King has no intention of giving up so easily. It's never been his way to act like that. I think he wants to use you for his own purposes, by whatever means necessary. He might try to force you to support him by threatening your life, or ours. He may put us in prison, or even kill us. Don't trust him!" said Eli.

Daniel had said nothing up till now, and he spoke hesitantly.

"It may be that the King hasn't repented, but we can't afford to scorn him. That would only let him brand us as hypocrites and liars, and maybe gain him sympathy among the people. That won't do, either."

"The King is crafty, and I don't doubt he set up this situation very carefully. We can't allow him to get credit for hypocrisy, but on the other hand we shouldn't despise him, either. I think we should tell him to come here publicly, quite alone, and answer for himself. I will give him my personal guarantee for his safety. Then we'll see what he chooses to do. If he refuses to come, it won't be because he didn't have a chance," said Jeremy.

They called for the King's messenger and gave him their answer, telling him to return to the King immediately. For a minute Jeremy was reminded of sending messengers from his office in Lord Amagon's house, and he was briefly filled with regret for the simplicity of his life in those days. He had learned some time ago that his old master had died in prison in the dungeons of Rustrum, and he wondered what had become of the House in Cerise, and all his friends there. He knew that Amagon had been a young man, with no children yet. It would be sad, if all his good work should fall apart and come to nothing. Jeremy decided that the fate of Cerise would be one of the things he demanded an accounting for, when the King should appear.

That did not happen immediately, however. Several days passed with no word from the King, and Jonah especially began to suspect some devilry was brewing. But even in the midst of their suspicion, when the trap was sprung it managed to catch all of them by surprise. On the tenth day since the King's messenger had been sent back to Rustrum, the King made his answer.

In the middle of the night, the boys were wakened by shouts and sounds of fighting outside the house. Jeremy had dreaded this very thing since giving the King his choice. He leaped from his bed and shouted for the others to get up as he threw on yesterday's clothes. Then he rushed to the bedroom window to find out what was going on, rubbing the sleep from his eyes and trying to wake up. He didn't need to look behind him to know the others were there.

There was no one else in the house at night except the four of them. They had agreed from the very beginning not to have any servants in the house, partly because of the danger of spies and traitors, and partly because they didn't think themselves above caring for their own needs. The old house was a sturdy one, with no windows on the ground floor and other features designed to make it highly defensible. The boys had made it a point to lock and barricade the doors every night, just in case of such an attack.

They looked down on the street outside to find hordes of soldiers surrounding the house. Several of them had cut down a tree and lopped off the branches to make a crude battering ram, which they were smashing against the front door. The door was strong, and it would take the King's men some time to break in, but their eventual success was beyond doubt. From the screams and sounds of fighting that could be heard through the walls, the army was brutally crushing all resistance in the town outside. It would be a matter of minutes before they broke into the house and either captured or killed all of them. Jeremy knew there was no time to waste.

"Come up to the roof," he told them urgently. All four of the boys ran up the main staircase to the third floor of the big house. The small door leading up onto the roof was locked, of course, but Jonah had the keys. Once everyone was through, he  locked it again behind them.`

"Maybe that will slow them down a little," he said, without much hope.

They scrambled up a narrow flight of steps and burst out onto the flat rooftop, breathless from running. They were hidden from the street by the false front of the house, but that wouldn't save them for long. There was no way down except for the steps they had just come up, and the two houses on either side were much too far away to reach by jumping. Fires were burning all over the town, filling the air with the acrid smell of smoke. The sound of fighting came from near and far. Jeremy looked sad.

"I never meant it to come to this," he murmured. None of them knew anything to say to that. Daniel, the least skilled in words but also the softest of heart, put an arm around his friend's shoulders. Jeremy smiled.

"Thank you all, for standing here with me till the end. I don't think it's quite time to despair just yet, but it may well be that not all of us survive till the morning. If that be so, then I want you all to know how dear you've been to me," he said. The others could only nod.

"We're not maggot food yet," Eli said fiercely, and Jeremy actually laughed.

"No, not yet, Eli. I have one thing yet to try, before it comes to that. I suggest you all lie down, or at least sit," he advised them. Then he sighed, almost too quietly to hear, stepped closer to the false front of the house, turned his face up to the sky full of stars, and raised his hands to pray.

Almost instantly, it seemed, the night sky was filled with dark clouds, and rain began to stream down upon the city, lightly at first, and then more and more heavily. At first the others wondered at this, because it seemed to them that hardened soldiers might curse the rain, but would certainly not be stopped by it. However, as the rain thickened into a torrent pouring down upon them, filling every street with deep water and making the very timbers of the house shake beneath them with the violence of the flood, they began to believe. The storm became so powerful, they couldn't bear to lift their heads from the rooftop. The drops came down stinging like needles, and they were amazed that Jeremy could continue to stand at all.

None of them slept that night, and it seemed a very long time till the sun rose.

## Chapter Ten
### Decisions

When the watery light of morning came, they expected to look out on a scene of devastation, but instead, they found the city not much changed from the day before, except for a few puddles and bits of mud. There were no soldiers, no destroyed houses, nor anything else to suggest the violence of the night, except a few burned-out buildings. They looked at Jeremy, who only smiled tiredly.

"The Most High has blessed us with a miracle," he said, answering the question they hadn't asked.

"It won't be long before word of all this gets back to the King, and to tell the truth, I'm too worn out to think about what he may do, then. We have at least a few hours before the next attack, whatever form it may take. Until then, I think I'll sleep a while. I suggest you all do the same," Jeremy said. With no more ado, he stumbled down the stairs and into the house, and collapsed onto the first bed he came to. (It was Eli's, in fact, but the younger boy didn't grudge it to him). The others found such resting places as they could, fully intending to sleep most of the day.

It was not to be.

Only a couple of hours later, they were awakened by pounding on the front door. Not soldiers this time, but leaders of the town. They had spent the night in terror of the King's army and then of the flood, and now they had finally plucked up enough courage to leave their homes. They demanded to see the Prophet. The front doors of the house were wrecked and splintered from the attack, and it took all four boys to shove the twisted hinges open just enough to let the guests come in. The doors had been on the very verge of collapsing when the flood came. Another five minutes and the King's men would have been inside the house. Jeremy knew the doors would have to be repaired immediately in case of another attack, but that was something he didn't have the energy to think about right now.

He let Jonah handle most of the questions from the townsfolk, only speaking himself when there was something the other boy couldn't answer. It took a long time to satisfy them, and when the last one was finally pushed out the door, it was getting close to evening again.

Jeremy gathered them all together in the kitchen soon afterward.

"We have to think of what's best to do now," he said, getting right to the point.

"The King has committed himself to fighting us, and he won't change his mind now. In a way that's more dangerous, because it lets him act openly against us, instead of having to pretend to think about what we say. On the other hand, he's lost the chance to fool us about his intentions," Jeremy said.

"I think we should go to Rustrum immediately and destroy him!" Eli said. "His treachery is proved beyond doubt, and a flood like the one last night will be the end of him."

"Maybe. . . but the Most High doesn't dispense miracles just because they might be helpful, Eli," Jonah scolded him, "Prophets have been killed many times before, as I'm sure I don't need to remind you."

"That may be so, Jonah, but whatever might be ahead, I'm not afraid of it," Eli said.

"Who said anything about being afraid?" Jonah snapped, beginning to scowl.

"Stop, please," Jeremy pleaded with them. "It's hard enough to think about these things, without the two of you fighting about it. Both of you have gone through so much for the sake of your friendship with me, so please, if you love me, keep peace between yourselves." Eli and Jonah were abashed by his words, and immediately apologized to each other.

"What do you think, Daniel?" Jeremy asked, looking at the youngest boy. He bit his lip and glanced at Eli and Jonah before he reluctantly answered.

"I think we should make sure the whole country knows what happened here. The King showed us he's no better than a criminal, attacking us in the middle of the night with no warning like that. He must have lost a good many of his best soldiers, too. The people in Rustrum know he isn't their only hope of survival anymore. In fact, they know the only reason they don't have rain is because of him. I think it cost the King a lot of support when his attack on us failed. People won't fear him as much anymore. It may be if we simply wait, then the people will throw him down on their own," he suggested hopefully. Jeremy smiled.

"You have a gentle heart, Daniel, and that's a gift from the Most High, and a good way to be.

Everything you say is true, but I think in this case we may need to act more forcefully. I'm afraid, if we give him time to recover from his loss, the King is well able to prepare another attack on us, and the next one might be successful. Even yesterday, if the door hadn't been locked, or if the soldiers had been able to break into the house quietly, without waking us, they could have captured or killed us while we slept, and that would have been the end of it. As Jonah pointed out, prophets have been killed before," Jeremy said. The others sat quietly, chewing on this.

"Are you saying we should march to Rustrum right away, and attack the King in his own palace?" Jonah asked.

"Maybe we should. I'm not sure, Jonah. If I only knew for sure," Jeremy said, even more quietly than before. His grim words and sadness were beginning to worry the others.

"Are you all right, Jeremy?" Daniel finally asked.

"No, not really," Jeremy admitted. "I always thought I wanted to do something awesome and grand, but I guess I never thought about what that might mean. Now the Most High has seen fit to lay on my shoulders a task which is beyond my strength and wisdom to accomplish. I'm tired, and I'm afraid, and I don't know what the best thing to do might be, and so much depends on the choices I make. So my heart is heavy, and there are times when I wish I'd never been called to this path." He looked at the others with sorrow in his eyes, which they could do nothing to soften.

"We would help you bear it, if we could," Daniel said.

"I know you would, Daniel, and that's a comfort to me, but sometimes there are things we can only do alone, if at all," Jeremy replied. Then he seemed to bring his thoughts back to the task at hand.

"I think we need to do something big, and soon. The King's attack yesterday can't be allowed to go unanswered. It was wicked, and if we fail to do anything about it, then we become hypocrites also," Jeremy said, drumming his fingers on the table.

"There's always the possibility of marching in strength with the army to Rustrum, rallying the citizens there, and overthrowing the King. That might seem like the easiest way, but I'm not sure it would be the best. For one thing, there are many soldiers still loyal to the King, and Rustrum is not easily taken. Nor do I wish to harm the people there. Even if we succeeded, there's still the problem of what comes next. We would be left with no King at all, and that's dangerous.

It might be that an even worse man could slip in and take Joseph's place. I've been thinking and praying carefully about that," Jeremy explained. Here he hesitated for a moment.

"The inscription inside the temple in Thaloth mentioned both a prophet and a King. You're to replace King Joseph," he said, looking at Jonah. He didn't wait to see how his old friend would react to that bit of news before turning at once to the others.

"You other two are free to do as you like, of course. The Most High has his own plans for you, and he hasn't shown them to me yet, as he has for Jonah. Cerise will need a leader also, and it may be that one of you is called to go back there. But whatever may happen, I know there are important things for you both to do, if you'll wait a little while to see what those may be," he told them.

"And what about you?" Daniel asked quietly.

"I make no plans for myself. I'll go where I'm called, and I don't know yet where that may be. I can only wait, and listen for the word of the Most High. As do we all," Jeremy answered. Then he became brisk.

"Now that all that's settled, I think it would be wise to tell the people at once, so there are no surprises. It will earn us the undying hatred of King Joseph and all who support him, of course, but that can't be helped. He had his chance to repent, and rejected it. Now he'll be replaced."

Jeremy turned to Jonah (who for once was quite speechless) and studied him briefly.

"You'll be a good King, I think. Have faith, old friend. From now on, I leave to you the conduct of the war. I'll help you when I can, but I have work of my own to do, to bring life back to the land, and to call the people back to righteousness."

"The people won't follow anyone but you, Jeremy," Jonah said, looking levelly at his friend.

"They'll follow anyone I command them to follow. You're the choice of the Most High, and if they reject you, they'll face His wrath," Jeremy said sternly.

There was nothing to be said to that, and Jeremy called an assembly of the people the very next afternoon, to be held in the largest square of Xanthus. In the meantime, clothes were chosen for Jonah, and a circlet of gold made for him, with a single diamond set on the forehead. That was the symbol of the King of Rustrum, who wore no crown.

At the assembly, Jeremy spoke powerfully against the wickedness of the King, and declared that the Most High had removed from him all authority, and replaced him with another more righteous man. He lifted up the circlet of gold for all to see, and a hush fell on the crowd. There were many people who expected him to set the circlet on his own head, and were surprised when he didn't do so. He turned to Jonah, who walked slowly forward in the blue robes of the King, and knelt with bowed head at Jeremy's feet. Jeremy put his right hand on Jonah's head to bless him, and then rubbed a drop of sweet oil on his forehead with one thumb. At the last, he whispered a few words of encouragement in his friend's ear, before he gently set the circlet of Rustrum on his head. Jeremy reached down to take Jonah's hand to help him to stand, where he faced the people for the first time. The hush continued for a moment, until Jeremy cried "Behold your King!", and the crowd erupted into wild cheers and applause.

Jonah's first act in his new office was to speak to the people, of course. He declared that the time had come to march to Rustrum, and remove the wicked King Joseph forever. More cheers were heard at that. Jonah went on, for he could be a powerful speaker when he chose to be.

Jeremy, as quietly as possible, slipped away from the center of attention and returned to the house. It would be a long time, most likely, before Jonah and the others returned from the assembly, and for a little while Jeremy wanted some peace and silence. He still had doubts about how things might turn out, and what the future might bring.

The house was empty as always, though he knew that would soon have to change. It was one thing for a wandering prophet and his friends to live alone and take care of themselves— it was quite another thing for the King to live like that. At the least, there would be servants and councilors and messengers coming to and fro almost constantly, and that would destroy the peace they had enjoyed. Jeremy sighed.

He walked quietly up to the third floor, and opened the little door that led out onto the roof. He came out into the bright sunshine of an autumn day, and stood there in silence for a minute, to feel the breeze against his face. He couldn't be sure, but he thought he detected the faint scent of salt on the wind. It reminded him of Rustrum down by the sea, and the struggle ahead.

He went to the west side of the building and sat down there with crossed legs to pray and seek guidance. He wondered if his friends had any idea how little he knew, and how often he was at a loss. He doubted they did. He was certain that choosing Jonah to replace King Joseph was the right thing to do, but he wasn't so sure what the Most High might have in mind for the other two. Nor even for himself, for that matter.

He was still praying when, hours later, the others came back to the house. Jonah had many new problems and cares to occupy his mind, and so perhaps it wasn't surprising that he didn't think to come looking for Jeremy. Nor did Eli, for he had been asked to begin the difficult process of choosing a few trusted servants for the house.

It was Daniel who finally came up to the rooftop and found Jeremy sitting by the retaining wall. Usually he would have left Jeremy alone at such a time, but at that moment the older boy looked up at him and smiled.

"Come here, Daniel," he asked, waving an arm at him. Daniel crossed the rooftop easily enough, and sat down facing Jeremy, with his legs crossed under him much like his friend was sitting.

"Did you want to talk to me, Jeremy?" he asked, when nothing was said.

"Yes I did, Daniel. I've been praying to the Most High, and I've learned some things the rest of you need to know. You remember when I spoke to you earlier, I said that you and Eli might think about going back to Cerise, and leading that city? The Most High has given that work to Eli. He came from the streets, and he knows the needs of that people more clearly than any of us others do. He's been a good and faithful servant in little things. Therefore, the Most High has said that he is to be placed over all of Cerise, to be the guardian and protector and Father of that city," Jeremy said.

"I know he'll do well there," Daniel nodded.

"As for me, the Most High has directed that I go up into the Cesmean Mountains, to the Lachishite barbarians, and preach to them, and you're to come with me. I don't know why, but there's some part for you to play with those people. Our work in Rustrum is almost done for now. Jonah and Eli will care for the people and their needs very well, and the Most High will remove the curse of the drought which has laid the land in ruins. We need fear no further for the people here," Jeremy explained.

Daniel didn't find these words completely comforting. The Lachishites of the mountains were a tale of terror to every child in Cerise, with good reason. Their cruelty was legendary. The idea of going to such a place scared him, but he said nothing.

"Don't worry. . .we won't leave the others for some time yet. At least not until Rustrum is captured, and King Jonah is safely in control of the land. Until then, things will go on very much as they have been doing. Don't say anything to the others about these things just yet, because I want to speak to them both together later this evening, when we can be alone," Jeremy told him. Daniel nodded again.

Jeremy stood up, and the other boy did likewise.

"Let's go down into the house and find something to eat and drink, Daniel. I'm exhausted and hungry after spending all day up here," Jeremy suggested. With that, they both went down into the house.

## Chapter Eleven
### Parting

The rest of the war concerned Jeremy very little, for it was a matter handled for the most part by Jonah and the leaders of the army. Jeremy had his own problems to deal with during this time. By the time Jonah approached the city of Rustrum at the head of an army of ten thousand men of the outlands, the people of the city rose in revolt against the remainder of King Joseph's guard, and slew both them and the King in the courtyard of the palace, and threw open the gates of the city to King Jonah with cheers and thanksgiving. For the most part. There were doubtless those who regretted the fall of the old king and hated his replacement, and Jonah would have his hands full for many years rooting out the last of these holdouts. But for now, the whole country was given up to rejoicing, and Jeremy pronounced an end to the drought, and for many days the blessed rain came down, until every river was full, and the grass began to grow thick and green in the fields. For many, it was the first sight of so much water that they had ever seen.

Eli eagerly accepted his task in Cerise, when he was told. He was sorry for the passing of Amagon, but even that couldn't erase his enthusiasm for the work that was given to him. Cerise would be richly blessed, with such a leader. Indeed, he chafed at the need to remain in Rustrum until things could be set in order, so anxious was he to be gone.

All told, the four of them remained together in Rustrum in the palace of the King for almost six months. By then, Jonah had begun to feel secure in his position, and a little more comfortable with it. He was indeed, as Jeremy had known he would be, a wise and faithful King.

But as time went on, Jeremy felt more and more the call of his other work that wasn't yet done. On a day when the first flowers of spring were blooming in the garden, he found Jonah in a moment of solitude, walking among the roses.

"You need to move on, don't you?" Jonah asked him sadly.

"Yes, I do. There's another task I'm called to do, and the Most High has allowed us a long while together, but now I know the time has come to begin my other work," Jeremy said. There was no point in denying it. Jonah chewed on that for a minute.

"Where will you go?" he finally asked.

"To the Lachishites first, and then. . . I can't say where, after that. But the Most High has revealed to me that there is a greater enemy abroad than Joseph who was King. He was the least of it, my friend. Indeed, it may be that we saved the land from one enemy, only to be destroyed by a worse one," Jeremy replied. Jonah looked a bit pale at that, and gripped Jeremy's hand.

"Tell me what you know, then! All these dark hints and suggestions cause me more fear than if I knew for certain that an army of ghouls stood outside the gates," Jonah cried.

"I don't know anything for certain," Jeremy protested. "That information hasn't been given to me yet. Be at ease! If it were necessary for us to know right now, then the Most High would have shown it to us. Since he hasn't, then it must be that the knowledge wouldn't serve our good, just now."

"I know," Jonah said, quite softly. Jeremy put a hand on his friend's shoulder.

"Don't be sad, Jonah. You'll lead the people well, and be a beloved King. The great enemy, whoever he may be, is not for you to fight. At least not yet. For now, that task belongs to me, and maybe to Daniel. You still have great works to do, yourself. Be faithful in what is asked of you. It will never be more than you can do," Jeremy told him.

Jonah looked unhappy.

"I know that, too," he said, "but it doesn't keep me from missing my friends. You don't realize, maybe, how lonely this palace can be. I'm King to all who see me, but never just Jonah anymore. A man would have to be insane to wish for a task like this. Must I really do it all alone?" he asked.

Jeremy thought about this for a minute.

"It may be that someday, when all is said and done, that our four paths will lead us back here. It well may be. . . but I don't know, Jonah. I keep the hope of it, but I can't forsake the task of the Most High," Jeremy said, heavily.

"No, you mustn't do that. I know you have your own path, and I have mine, and it couldn't be otherwise. But I never said I had to like it," Jonah said, with an effort to be cheerful. He took a deep breath and went on.

"Take whatever things you need from the city stores, and from any town inside the kingdom along the way to. . . wherever you're going. Go with my blessing, and be certain that the sooner you return, the better it will please me," Jonah said seriously. He kissed his friend's signet ring, as even a King might do with one he thought greater than himself, and they parted for that time.

It was a long while before they saw each other again.

*Part II*

## Chapter Twelve
### Kalavah

Jeremy and Daniel rode slowly through the wilds of the Cesmean Mountains, in a pouring thunderstorm. Jeremy had often thought, during the past three years since they left Rustrum, that it would have been very useful sometimes to have been granted the power to *halt* a storm, instead of bringing one down. The Mountains were windy and cold, full of wet mists and dark dripping rocks. The two boys were never completely dry at any time, and soaking wet as often as not.

The Lachishite barbarians had been hostile at first, thirsting for Jeremy's blood to drink in honor of

Marithe and Cesme, their hateful gods. He and Daniel had been obliged to defend themselves several times, and on one occasion they had been ambushed by a horde of attackers and come close to death. Jeremy's prayer to the Most High had brought down a scourge of lightning upon the barbarians and killed many of them before the others fled. After that experience, word had spread quickly among the mountain tribes that here was a man dangerous to touch, and for the most part they had been left alone since then.

The mountain folk had few permanent villages, and such as there were, the boys encountered only by chance, for there was no one to ask directions of. These villages most often centered around some ancient grove of black oak trees held sacred to the worship of Marithe. Invariably nearby were the rings of hewn black stone given over to the blood worship of Cesme, at Midsummer, and the Elsinore, and other of the accursed days celebrated by these people.

Whenever he came to such places, Jeremy destroyed them utterly, setting fire to the groves and breaking the rings of stone, so they could never again be used. The people had been awe-struck by his power over the heavens, and had wanted at first to make him into a god as well. He cursed their blasphemy and preached to any who would listen to repent of their ignorant wickedness and follow the Most High. Some of the Lachishites had been convinced, and these he spent a while teaching and protecting until he felt they could be strong in the face of temptation to slide back into the old ways. Then he and Daniel would move on to another place.

So it had gone on for some time now, and the mountains were dotted with little groups of converted villages. Only a handful, to be sure, for Jeremy couldn't be everywhere at once, and the teaching and strengthening of each village took time. Indeed, the conversion of the Lachishites was the work of a lifetime, or more than a lifetime.

He and Daniel were staying in the village of Kalavah, deep in an isolated valley. It had an icy stream that fed from the glaciers higher up, and just enough flat land to support a few little farms where the people grew barley and potatoes. Not much else would grow in such a cold place.

It was one of the larger villages they had converted, with almost five hundred people who lived in the valley, and Jeremy and Daniel both taught from the Book of the Prophets each day in the largest hut. They never lacked for a crowd, as often as they opened the doors. Of all the villages they had visited, Kalavah had received them the most warmly.

Jeremy had taken a quiet half hour before the teaching was to begin to gather his thoughts and pray, when a soft knock came at the door.

"Come in," he said, and looked up to see Daniel. He'd grown so tall in the past few months, he almost banged his head on the door frame as he came in.

"Jeremy, there's something I'd like to talk to you about," the younger boy said.

"What is it, Daniel?" he asked absentmindedly, looking back down at his book. He was thinking how to go about explaining a particularly difficult part of the text, and his thoughts were far from the present moment.

Daniel hesitated, as if not sure how to begin. He scuffed his feet on the floor and twisted the hem of his sleeve. It made him seem nervous, and Jeremy wondered very much at that. He put away his other work and focused all his attention on the younger boy.

"Jeremy, we've gone through a lot of difficult times together, and done so many wonderful things. You're my best friend, and always will be," he began, awkwardly.

Jeremy didn't entirely like the drift of this conversation, and when Daniel hesitated again, he spoke.

"I can see you want to tell me something you're afraid I might not like. But come, you know there need be no secrets between you and me. Tell me what's on your mind," he encouraged. Daniel looked only a little less uncomfortable, but Jeremy watched him take a deep breath.

"Well, the thing is this. Tabitha and I have been talking a lot, these past few months, and I think," he began, and stopped again when he saw his friend smiling. So *that* was it, Jeremy thought to himself.

"I think you're trying to tell me you love this girl, and so now everything looks different to you. Is that it?" he asked, quietly.

"Yes," Daniel answered.

"That's not really unexpected, maybe. She's a beautiful girl, and very intelligent and good of heart, too. And her devotion to the Most High is the greatest we've yet seen among all these people," Jeremy said. He felt like kicking himself for overlooking the situation so long.

"I want to marry her," Daniel said abruptly. Jeremy had to chew on that for a few minutes before he could think of any good answer.

"You're a little young to be thinking of that," he observed mildly.

"I'm sixteen. That's not too young among the Lachishites," Daniel pointed out. When Jeremy didn't deny this, Daniel went on.

"I've prayed earnestly to the Most High, and so has Tabitha, and we believe it's our appointed task to preach to her lost people and save them from their wickedness."

"I see," Jeremy said, a little absently. His thoughts were turned inward, to see if perhaps the Most High would give him wisdom concerning this matter. But he felt in his heart, already, that Daniel had spoken the truth. He opened his eyes and looked at the younger boy soberly.

"Again I see the wisdom and the kindness of the Most High. If I had known, in Rustrum, the task He meant for you, I don't know if I could have found the strength to bring you here. It would have seemed a grief greater than I could have borne at that time, to leave the gentlest and kindest of my friends to spend his life in a land of cruelty and filth. I see now that you've spoken the truth. You've learned so much strength and wisdom, without losing the kind heart you always had. I bless you with all happiness that it lies within me to give, my friend," Jeremy told him. Daniel looked taken aback.

"Leave me?" he asked, with wide eyes.

"Yes. . . you have your purpose now, Daniel, and it might be that a kind heart is needed most in a land that has seen so little of that. I've wondered for a long time why the Most High sent me to this place. I see now that my purpose in coming was to bring you here, and to teach and lead you to the point that you were ready to take up your life's work. My task here is done now, and yours is just beginning. Whereas I. . . the Most High has other work for me, already," Jeremy explained. He couldn't bear to look at Daniel while he said this, for it wasn't at all what he wanted, and the thought of going out alone in the world after losing his last friend was daunting. Daniel said nothing for a few minutes.

"I hoped you might stay here with us. The people listen to you so much better than they do to Tab or me," he finally said. Jeremy knew what he really meant by this was that he wasn't sure if he could handle such a big task by himself.

"The Most High will be with you. He never would have given you this task, if He didn't know already that you could bear it," he said. Daniel scuffed his feet on the floor again and couldn't quite meet his eyes.

"You really think so?" he finally asked.

"Certainly," Jeremy said.

"Do you know where you'll go, then?" Daniel asked.

"No, not yet. All I know is to go down out of the mountains, on the north side. Then I'll see what there is to see," Jeremy explained.

"The north side? Are you sure? Nobody lives up that way, not even Lachishites. There's nothing there but wilderness," Daniel pointed out.

"True enough. I have no idea what the reason for going there might be. But I do know there's another enemy somewhere, one much worse than King Joseph, and so far I've done nothing to fight him. I think he may be there, in the north. So I feel in my heart," Jeremy replied. Daniel furrowed his brow and chewed on his lower lip, a nervous habit he always fell back on when he was worried.

"What if you get hurt, or you can't find the way through? You'd have no one to help you," Daniel said.

"I think I'll be fine," Jeremy assured him.

"You can't know that. Nobody goes into the wilderness alone, Jeremy. It's not safe, and it's not safe to fight an enemy alone, either," Daniel insisted. Jeremy sighed. This wasn't a discussion he wanted to have right now. It was hard enough to leave already. He knew Daniel meant well, but at the moment it wasn't helping. He had to go, and that was that.

"Do you have another suggestion, then? I have to go, and you have to stay, and I don't see any way around that," Jeremy said firmly. That silenced the argument, as he knew it would, but Daniel still looked unhappy.

"I'm just worried about you, that's all. But as a matter of fact I do have an idea. Me and Tab could come with you, at least until you get to the other side of the mountains. Then we could come back here. Our work can wait that long," he suggested.

Jeremy thought about this, looking deep into his heart to see what the will of the Most High might be.

"I have a strong feeling that wouldn't be a good idea, Daniel," he said, seriously.

"Why not?" Daniel asked.

"I just don't think it would be wise, that's all," Jeremy insisted. Daniel looked as if he were ready to argue the point some more, but then he seemed to have a change of heart.

"Do as you must, then," he said, resigned. Jeremy smiled.

"Don't worry, Daniel. It will all work out as it should, and I'll take no more risks than I have to," he promised. So the conversation ended.

Jeremy left Kalavah soon afterwards. He left his copy of the Book of the Prophets with Daniel, for he and Tabitha to use in their work. There were tears from some of the Lachishites on the morning when he departed, but also smiles, for they knew he left them only to further serve the Most High. The people joined hands to sing a hymn of blessing and thanksgiving, which he could hear for a long while as he climbed the steep wall of the valley.

He emerged onto a blinding white snowfield, glistening and shining in the sun. The footing was treacherous, forcing him to pay close attention to where he stepped. He carried a stout oak staff in his right hand, to probe for hidden cracks and crevasses ahead of him, and also to help keep him from slipping on the ice. The Lachishites used them frequently, and Jeremy had been in the mountains long enough that he would have felt almost naked without a staff.

It took most of the day for him to reach the opposite side of the glacier, though it wasnt't very wide. The glaring light stung his eyes and made them water, and there was a gusty wind that made the ice even harder to walk on than it would have usually been. By the time he reached the north side of the ice, the short autumn day was almost gone, leaving him to fumble his way on through the gathering dusk. He was glad to feel solid rock under his boots again, for he knew very well how dangerous the ice could be even at the best of times.

He was high above the little valley of Kalavah now; he could make it out only as a dim crack in the twilight far below him. As soon as he walked a little farther he would cross the ridge top, and then he knew he would likely never see that village, nor Daniel, ever again. He paused a minute to look down and say good-bye, and suddenly felt more lonely than he had in years.

The chill wind kept him from lingering too long. There was little shelter to be found high in the mountains, but he knew he would have to locate somewhere to spend the night before it got too late. People had been known to freeze to death in the high places. It wasn't quite that cold just yet, but he knew it soon would be, after the sun went down.

There was no path to be followed, for no one came to those places often enough to make one, not even animals. The whole world was bare jagged rocks and bits of snow and ice, with nothing alive except ragged gray lichen. Jeremy picked his way through the rocks and scree as well as he could manage. He knew he was headed generally northward, for he could look at the dull afterglow of the setting sun and tell that much.

Not long after dark, he found a sort of hollow in a rock face. It wasn't really deep enough to be called a cave, just a scooped out spot that might keep off the wind a little bit. Jeremy had seen no other places that might do better, so he decided to make camp in the little hollow for the night. He had made it over the ridge top and a little way down the northern side into the next valley before night fell completely. It was a bit warmer there, and less windy.

He built a fire from some of the gnarled willow and pine shrubs that grew here and there on the mountainside in that place, then ate a little food and wrapped himself in every blanket he possessed.

It was the first time in a long while that Jeremy had travelled alone. He was used to having someone to talk to in the long evenings, and he didn't much like the solitude. He almost wished he'd allowed Daniel and Tabitha to come with him, after all.

He lay quietly in the hollow, looking up at the stars and thinking. Nothing disturbed him, except the occasional pop and crackle of the fire. He remembered, idly, that it would be his birthday in a few weeks. Twenty-one years old, he would be. In Cerise, that was the year when a boy was expected to move on to something new. He would have had to retire as pagemaster at that age, if he'd remained all this time in

Amagon's house. He didn't suppose it mattered much, now.

All the same, he felt in his bones that a change was coming; some new thing in his life that he'd never dealt with before. He felt it as surely as he felt the warmth of the fire against his face. He didn't know what it might be yet, and at the moment he was too tired to care.

He did feel a great satisfaction to be back on the trail of the Great Enemy again. He hadn't forgotten his last words to Jonah before he left Rustrum, and the still-unknown danger to his friends had nagged him the whole time he spent with the Lachishites. Now, he felt that the Most High had set him back on the path of hunting down the real danger, and in his heart of hearts he was happy, in spite of the cold and lonely journey.

He spent a little time praying, but he was so tired from crossing the ice that he fell asleep before he finished.

## Chapter Thirteen
### *The Lake of Fire*

Jeremy went on through the rough and broken mountains for several weeks without seeing anything worth mentioning. There were no people, and not many animals. He might rarely see an eagle wheeling overhead in the cold blue sky, and he wondered how the birds kept from starving in such a desolate country. He was footsore and tired from the hard rocks and the cold wind that never ceased. Just yesterday he'd had to cross another glacier in a narrow valley, and almost broken his ankle when he stepped into a snow-filled crack in the surface. It was still painful and bruised.

He thanked the Most High it hadn't been any worse, but it still slowed him down.

Today, as he limped along, he thought he saw yet another ice field some distance ahead of him. It was a bright whiteness that reflected the sunlight, and from what he could tell, filled an entire valley. Jeremy gritted his teeth in disgust and glanced to either side to see if there might be any way to avoid crossing the ice.

There was not. To the west was a rock-strewn slope so steep and sheer it could almost qualify as a cliff. He knew better than to try climbing it, for if he dislodged even one of the smaller stones it might set off a rock slide that could kill him. Better to leave that alone.

The east was no better, though. On that side the slope dropped down into a muddy bog that went on as far as he could see. There seemed to be no shortage of bogs in places where any flat land existed. This one was full of blood-sucking *kronatsiya* plants, with barbed thorns as sharp and strong as steel needles. Jeremy recognized their pale little flowers and prickly skin even from a distance, for they were one of the first things he and Daniel had had to learn to avoid when they came to the mountains. The plants looked harmless, until you got too close. Then a hundred barbed thorns lashed out and buried themselves deep in the flesh of the unlucky victim. Each thorn was still attached to the mother plant by a thin tube, through which the plant immediately began to drain the victim of blood. The thorns couldn't be removed without tearing flesh and making a hideous wound. Because of that, even people who'd been lucky enough to be rescued from the plant itself often died from the wounds and blood loss. The *kronatsiya* wasn't common, being found only in boggy places with lots of sun, but it made up for that in deadliness. Jeremy dared not go anywhere near them.

He sighed and resigned himself to crossing another ice floe. It probably wouldn't be the last time he encountered one, he thought.

He picked his way toward the white gleam, being careful to give the *kronatsiya* plants a wide berth. There was a fairly narrow passage between the cliff wall and the bog, maybe two hundred feet wide. He stayed as close to the cliff as possible. If it came right down to it, he thought he'd rather deal with a rock slide than with the blood-suckers.

As he got closer to the ice floe, he noticed that it didn't look like any ice he'd yet seen. It wasn't as shiny, and the surface seemed to undulate sluggishly like ocean swells. Jeremy became curious, and the closer he came the more certain he was of the movement.

He came abruptly to the edge of a truly immense valley that must have been five miles wide, and even longer than that lengthwise. The entire valley was filled almost to the brim, not with ice as he had thought, but with thick white mist. There was a fairly sharp line dividing the mist from the air, as if he were looking at a milk-white bay or lake.

Jeremy knelt down and touched the mist. It felt strangely warm, but there seemed to be nothing else unusual about it.

After a few minutes, he ventured to walk a little way down the slope of the valley until his head was under the surface of the mist. Here he found that it was possible to see several feet ahead, though it had looked impenetrable from above. He took another step downwards, and then another. There seemed to be few rocks, and he knew there wouldn't be any *kronatsiya* plants in a place with so little sunlight.

That didn't mean there might not be other dangers, though. He went on as quietly and carefully as he possibly could, straining to listen to every sound, since he could see so little.

It continued to get warmer and warmer, the lower he went, until he began to sweat from the heat.

Suddenly, with no warning at all, he stepped into hot water. He leaped backward with a cry of surprise, but then came back to investigate. The water was on the verge of being too hot to tolerate, like a very hot bath. Vapors rose off the surface as he watched, and he guessed that was where the mist came from. He waded out into the water for some distance, and found that it quickly became even hotter than it had been near the shore, so that he was in danger of being scalded. He retreated to the bank to think.

He wasn't sure how to get around the lake, or river, or whatever it might be. The water would cook him alive if he tried to swim or wade, and he had no boat, nor any way to build one. He finally decided to follow the shoreline, and see if perhaps he might be able to come around the water that way.

There were no cat tails or willow trees or any of the other plants you might expect to find near water. Everything was rock and dirt, with a few patches of tough-looking grass. He didn't have too much trouble following the shore, which curved gradually and smoothly to the north-east. In places the water bubbled and smoked like a boiling kettle. Whenever he approached one of these places, the air grew so hot and humid it was almost unbearable. Fortunately such spots were uncommon.

He walked on for the rest of that day and most of the next without seeing anything new, but around mid afternoon he came to a place where the boiling water of the lake spilled out over a noisy little fall, and formed a river that departed for lands unknown. He walked a little way downstream and found that the river wasn't too much of an obstacle, for there were large rocks he could use as stepping stones to get across. Even if he did slip and fall in, the water had cooled considerably after running out of the lake.

He did cross, and on the far side he discovered a well-used path along the bank. That surprised him, for it was the first work of human hands he'd seen since leaving Kalavah.

It also worried him a bit. Who knew what kind of people might live in a place like that? He became extra watchful, stealing quietly along the path back toward the lake shore. The mist kept him from seeing or even hearing anything useful until he was very close, but he strained his ears anyway. Presently, the path brought him back to the steaming waterfall where the lake poured out into the rocky riverbed. Here, the path veered off to the north along the shore.

Jeremy stopped for a few minutes, uncertain of whether he really wanted to follow the path any farther. He didn't like not being able to see more than a few feet ahead. There wasn't really much danger of getting lost as long as he stayed on the path, but he kept feeling that something hideous was watching him, waiting to spring at him any moment from out of the mist. The hairs on the back of his neck were hackled, and refused to lay down again. There was nothing in particular to be seen, or heard, or smelt. . . nothing especially to put him on guard that he could tell, but his heart was pounding nevertheless.

There are times when we talk ourselves into doing things we know are foolish, and for Jeremy this was one of those times. He couldn't help thinking it was feeble and cowardly to turn aside when he didn't even know if any danger really existed or not. He convinced himself there was no reason to fear, in spite of his instincts, and proceeded cautiously along the path.

For a while, nothing happened. The path was broad and clear, and the sound of the falls faded gradually into the background behind him until silence reigned once more. There was an occasional bubbling noise from the hottest parts of the lake. He crept along as quietly and (he hoped) as inconspicuously as possible, for he still felt that oppressive sense of danger. Indeed, it became so strong that he had almost made up his mind to turn back after all, when he stumbled into the middle of the last thing in the world he would have expected to find in such a place.

A herd of goats was grazing on the lichens and willow shrubs and sparse grass that throve in the valley. Jeremy had no idea how many there were, for he could see only three or four at a time. They looked up at him curiously for a few seconds, then went back to nibbling the plants. None of them made any noise. Every animal he saw was pure white, almost invisible in the mist.

They were the first large animals he'd seen since leaving Kalavah, and he thought at first they were wild, until he noticed a white collar around the neck of one of them. When he looked more closely, he saw that all the goats were wearing white collars. They were hard to see against the animals' white fur.

While he was noticing these things, a set of steel-hard talons seized him from behind, and he found himself pulled instantly up into the sky. The ground vanished into the mist below him, and he could see nothing except the huge black claws that held him, vise-like, in their grip.

The mist dampened all sound, and Jeremy was held in such a way that he could neither hear nor see what it was that held him. He could only feel the tips of the thing's claws, sharp as needles, digging into his ribs.

It wasn't really very long before a gray cliff loomed up out of the mist, and Jeremy found himself dropped carelessly onto a wide stone ledge. He suffered no worse than a few scrapes and bruises, for the stone was mostly smooth. Whatever it was that had brought him to this place was nowhere to be seen, and for a little while Jeremy stood there rubbing his bruises and catching his breath. Presently, when nothing happened, he began to cautiously explore the ledge.

He was very careful about approaching the edge, for he had no idea how high up he might be, nor whether the edge was crumbly or not. It seemed to be solid stone, dropping sheer down into the mist. He followed it all the way around and found no way to get down off the ledge. On one side it joined the main cliff wall, and on that side also there was no way to escape. He couldn't tell how far up the cliff might go above the ledge, and there were no handholds or cracks he could use. He did find a trickle of water emerging from the rock wall, forming a puddle on the ledge before disappearing. The ledge was about forty feet deep and twice that distance in width. It was bare and featureless for the most part, except for the spring he had found. There was a sort of nest at one end, built of willow sticks and rushes and lined with what looked like goat skins.

The ledge was littered with old bones, some of them cracked and broken. He noticed tooth marks on several of these, and shivered. Whatever lived in this place was definitely a meat eater. He could tell the bones had come from goats, for the horns were still attached to several of them. That was not much comfort, though, because a creature big enough to eat a goat was certainly big enough to eat a human being. Bits of rotting flesh still clung to some of the bones, and there was a hideous stench of decay.

He retreated to the back of the ledge, feeling a little safer with a wall on at least one side of him. The thing might move silently through the mist, but at least now it wouldn't be able to snatch him from behind as it had done in the valley.

He still had his sword and his dagger, and that was something. Jeremy had no idea what he was up against yet, but he grimly decided to make it pay dearly for its next meal, if it came to that.

He took a drink of water from the spring, being careful to keep an eye out for the flying thing. It was cold on the ledge, and he knew he would soon need shelter, if he lived long enough. That thought was not a cheerful one, but Jeremy decided it was much too soon to give up yet. As Eli might have said, he wasn't maggot food yet. He explored the back of the ledge more thoroughly, discovering several narrow cracks in the stone. They weren't deep enough or big enough to be called caves, but Jeremy thought he could fit inside. In there, he might be out of reach of the flying thing's claws, he thought. He still had a little food in his pack, though he knew it wouldn't last more than a week or so at most. If he couldn't find a way down off the ledge by then, he would soon perish whether the flying thing got him or not.

Jeremy was definitely in a tight spot, but he made the best of it that he could. He refilled his water bottle at the spring, then retreated as deep as he could squeeze into the largest of the cracks in the wall. Before he did anything foolhardy he wanted more information about his enemy.

The thing that gave him the most hope were the goats in the valley. He'd seen the collars on each of them, and that sort of thing wasn't done by a brute beast. Nor did he think something with talons the size of swords could have done the delicate job of putting such things on the animals. There had to be people in the valley, somewhere, and surely this flying thing that devoured their goats was an enemy of theirs. He doubted they could reach the ledge any easier than he could get down from it, for if they could, wouldn't they already have come here and destroyed the flying thing? But, when he did get down (he refused to consider the other possibility), they might help him then.

Jeremy did have a rope, of course, but it was no more than a hundred feet long. He suspected the cliff was probably much higher than that, although he had no way to tell for sure without actually trying it. He was reluctant to do that until he knew where the flying thing was. It wouldn't do at all for it to come back and find him hanging off the cliff, helpless.

So he waited, for what seemed a very long time indeed.

## Chapter Fourteen
### Malchouk

Though it may sound difficult to believe, with the hideous danger he was in, Jeremy actually slept for a while in the crack. He didn't intend to, but maybe the long day and the ordeal with the flying thing are enough to explain it. In any case, he woke to find himself staring into a large black eye not ten feet from his face. He was so startled he cried out.

The eye blinked, and he heard a rough, juicy kind of laughter from outside the crack.

"You may as well come out of there, man-thing. I've had an excellent dinner already today, and I'm more curious than hungry. . . at least for now," a gravelly voice said. Then it laughed again.

Jeremy was not such a fool as to listen to this suggestion, of course, but on the other hand he didn't want to make the thing too angry just yet.

"I thank you for your kindness, sir, but I'm quite comfortable at the moment!" he called out.

"Suit yourself, runt," the thing replied, coming closer to peer at him again with that hideous eye. It was jet black, with no pupil, and larger than a dinner plate. It was surrounded by dirty gray scales.

"You're strange looking, for a man thing," the creature commented after a while. Then curiosity seemed to get the better of it. "Who are you, and where did you come from, and what are you doing in my valley?" it asked.

"Ah, sir, those questions would be long in the telling," Jeremy replied, trying to sound as mysterious as possible. "Might I ask the name of my host, before I begin?" he asked. The eye blinked, but the voice chuckled again.

"You may indeed. My name is Malchouk, the Master of the Lake of Fire, and those are my goats you were fiddling with earlier. None comes here without my invitation, and even fewer depart again," the voice laughed evilly. Jeremy began to be quite afraid of what he'd gotten himself into, but he hoped to play on Malchouk's curiosity.

"Great Malchouk, I come from the south far away, a journey of many years. I am the Prophet of the Most High, and I come here on orders that even the mightiest dare not hinder," he began.

"Oh, really?" Malchouk scoffed.

"Yes, indeed. The Most High has crushed the wicked King of Rustrum, and destroyed the groves of Marithe and Cesme. I come here to seek the Great Enemy and defeat him," Jeremy declared. Malchouk laughed again.

"You're a proud little rooster, aren't you? And what a shame it must be that such a grand story will end in Malchouk's belly before another day has gone! Then, when your bones lie rotting in the sun, we will see how great your lord is then!" he scorned.

"Have a care, Monster! If you dare blaspheme the Most High, you may not live to regret it," Jeremy warned sternly. There was a sharp intake of breath, as if Malchouk were shocked beyond belief.

"You dare threaten me?" he said, so angry he almost whispered the words.

"I threaten no one. But you should be glad I saved your life by warning you," Jeremy told him, mildly. That seemed to enrage the beast.

"We'll soon see about that," he hissed. There was a scrabbling movement outside, and soon Malchouk's razor-sharp talons entered the cave. Jeremy, his heart pounding, tried desperately to squeeze deeper into the crack. The talons came within inches of his belly before stopping. Malchouk could reach no farther, and he slashed at Jeremy in rage. Jeremy felt the air move from the slashing claws, but they couldn't quite come close enough to hurt him.

After a while, Malchouk gave up on this and withdrew his claws. His anger had cooled to the point of letting him speak rationally again.

"I may not be able to reach you, man thing, but that makes no difference. You will find death in there as surely as you will find it out here- only the timing is different!" Malchouk snarled. Then he seemed to get himself under control.

"Since you prefer a long, slow death to a quick and clean one, I will leave you to enjoy it," he declared. There was more noise from outside, and Malchouk seemed to go away.

Jeremy didn't trust this, and certainly not enough to emerge from the cave. Malchouk might be waiting to pounce on him just outside.

If he was, then he was disappointed that night. Jeremy ate and drank a little, then settled as comfortably as he could into the crack and slept again.

Jeremy spent almost a week in this way, until his water and food began to run very low indeed. From time to time Malchouk would come to the crack and look to see if he was still alive, his big black eye almost filling the opening. Such times were always in the evening, just before dark. Jeremy began to suspect that the creature was away during most of the daylight hours and returned to the ledge only to sleep at night, but he dared not test his guess.

Sometimes Malchouk would talk to him, and amongst the curses and threats he gathered quite a bit of useful information. A small tribe of humans lived in the valley, tending Malchouk's goats and doing such other things as he commanded from time to time. They were (he said) in mortal terror of him, and he killed and ate one of them now and then just to keep the rest in line. They lived in caves on the north shore of the lake, and lived mostly on fish from the river.

Malchouk didn't seem to know (or care) much about anything beyond his valley. He hated the open air beyond the mist, and never went there if he could help it. The naked sun hurt his eyes and blinded him.

Jeremy said as little as possible to him during these conversations, hoping the monster would let slip something he could actually use. Fortunately, it wasn't difficult to keep him talking. Malchouk had a gift for gab that would have put an old woman to shame.

But the situation was beginning to get desperate, and Jeremy dared not delay much longer before trying to do something. Without food or water, he'd soon begin to get weak. Therefore he made a bold plan.

He stealthily removed his dagger from its sheath on his belt, testing the point to make sure it was sharp, and prayed for the best. In Cerise, he had had to study swordplay and self-defense, as did all the pages. That was part of what an "educated and noble" person of the city was expected to know. However, he had learned mostly with the broadsword, and the little dagger he carried was not his best weapon. He prayed that the short range would make up for his lack of skill.

That evening, when Malchouk came nosing around the cave and put his eye up to the opening to examine his captive, Jeremy was ready. He quickly let fly his dagger, and before Malchouk had time to move or even realize his danger, the blade was buried to the hilt in his eye.

He howled, and thrashed and bellowed in his fury and pain. As Jeremy had expected, the claws soon entered his cave again, as Malchouk in his fury tried to reach him again. Again he fell short by mere inches, and Jeremy took the opportunity to stab the vile arm with his sword. Malchouk howled again, and beat his tail against the cliff wall where Jeremy's cave was located, causing bits of dust and pebbles to come raining down on the boy's head.

After a while, all the noise ceased. Jeremy ventured close enough to the opening to get a good look outside. Malchouk was nowhere to be seen. This didn't surprise Jeremy, because he hadn't expected to kill the monster so easily as that. He was blinded in one eye, and probably wouldn't dare risk the other one by peering into Jeremy's cave again.

Still seeing nothing, Jeremy boldly stepped out into the open, keeping his back against the wall. He kept his sword at the ready, prepared for a sudden attack from any direction. The ground in front of his cave was smeared with blood and foul-smelling slime. His dagger was nowhere to be seen.

Jeremy didn't linger. He ran swiftly to the spring and refilled his water bottle, for thirst was the main danger he faced. That done, he returned quickly to the cave. He didn't know when (or if) Malchouk would return, and he didn't want to push his luck too far.

In fact, it was almost a whole day before Malchouk came back to the ledge. Jeremy heard him land on the stone outside, though he didn't dare approach the cave. Jeremy felt confident enough to stand closer to the opening now, and for the first time he got a good look at the creature.

Malchouk was a hideous beast, covered mostly in dirty gray scales, with a few bedraggled black feathers. He was most like a lizard, if you ignored the feathers and the huge leathery wings. He might have been a sort of dragon, though not like any Jeremy had ever heard of. His mouth was full of sharp teeth, many of which protruded from his lips even with his mouth shut. His right eye was a crusted ruin, covered in dried blood and still trickling slime. It was obviously destroyed.

There was nothing wrong with his left eye, though, for he soon spoke.

"I see you, man thing. You may as well come out. I've decided to let you go, if I have your promise to leave my valley and never return," Malchouk said.

Jeremy considered this. He was almost certain the evil creature was lying, but there was always the possibility that he might not be. Malchouk knew well enough that Jeremy would starve sooner or later, and then he would be rid of him. Surely he could sleep elsewhere for a month or so if he feared an attack in the dark. Jeremy knew he was not the kind of creature from whom pity could be expected, so therefore he had to have some plan up his scaly sleeve. Jeremy dared not accept his offer before he knew what that plan might be.

"Give me time to consider your offer," Jeremy told him. Malchouk bared his teeth in a kind of scowl.

"Consider carefully, man thing. My generosity may decline with time," he said.

Jeremy thought carefully indeed. He knew there was no way to get down off the ledge except by flying, and therefore Malchouk would have to be the one to take him down. But what if the faithless creature carried him high up in the air and then dropped him? And what about the people who tended the goats? Jeremy was reluctant to leave them enslaved. However, the first thing to do was to get down from the ledge.

"I accept your deal," Jeremy told him, emerging boldly from the cave. He held his sword at the ready, where he knew Malchouk could see it. The creature eyed him cautiously for a second.

"I will have to pick you up in my claws to carry you down," Malchouk told him at length.

"I think not, monster. Carry me on your back instead," Jeremy suggested.

"Very well, then," Malchouk agreed, kneeling on the ledge and turning somewhat away. Jeremy was a little surprised that the monster agreed so quickly. He kept his sword ready, and summoned all his courage to approach the monster. There was a fetid stench about the thing's wrinkled skin and feathers, like rotted meat. Jeremy carefully climbed up right between Malchouk's wings, in the very spot where he judged it would be hardest to drop him, and gripped a fold of skin tightly.

"Are you ready?" Malchouk asked irritably.

"Ready," Jeremy told him grimly. A second later, the beast dropped off the edge of the cliff.

After that first sickening plunge, Malchouk's flight was surprisingly smooth and silent. The mist parted quietly in front of him, and closed without a whisper behind. Jeremy couldn't tell if they were making any progress at all. Warm drafts of air rose up from below them, and Malchouk's wings hardly moved at all, riding the thermals.

Malchouk said nothing and seemed to pay him no attention, and as the flight went on Jeremy gradually loosened his death grip on the monster's skin.

But Malchouk's heart was black with treachery, and he felt the slackening hold quite well. He bided his time, circling in the mist, until he felt that just the right moment had come.

Then, with horrible speed, he plunged earthward and rolled over, trying to dislodge his rider.

In spite of his suspicion, Jeremy was caught off guard by the sudden change of direction and almost unseated. Indeed, he lost his grip on Malchouk's skin and fell completely off his back, and would have been lost entirely if he had not managed to grab a handful of black feathers just under the leading edge of the monster's wing. He held on as tightly as he could possibly grasp as Malchouk plunged and bucked, slamming him repeatedly against the underside of his wing and the side of his body.

Jeremy knew he couldn't hold on much longer. With a desperate prayer, he let go with one hand and reached for his sword. It isn't an easy thing to draw a sword when your body is being slammed in a dozen directions at once and you're holding on for dear life to only a clump of dirty feathers, but somehow he managed it. Then, with a tight grip, he plunged the sword point into Malchouk's scaly hide, just below the wing.

Malchouk screamed, and a gout of hot black blood gushed out of the wound. He stopped bucking, and began to descend. At first this seemed to be intentional, but soon Malchouk's wings buckled up and the dying monster began to fall uncontrollably.

Jeremy let go of his sword and grabbed the feathers with both hands again, trying to climb up onto Malchouk's back. He made it only a little way before both he and the monster's body plunged into the hot water of the lake.

He hit the surface with his body more or less vertical. Otherwise, the impact would probably have knocked him senseless at the very least, and that would have meant drowning. As it was, he plunged deep under the surface and wanted to scream from the pain. It was like being boiled alive in a huge cauldron. Malchouk's body floated back to the surface rapidly, and Jeremy climbed up as quickly as he could on top of it, to get out of the water. His skin was red and stinging over every inch of his body that he could feel, like a very bad all-over sun burn. He lay gasping in pain on Malchouk's back, unable to do anything to save himself.

The body floated aimlessly in the lake, and Jeremy had no way to paddle it or direct where it went. The air out on the surface of the lake was so hot and humid he almost couldn't breathe it. At times he could scoop up a little water from the lake in his bottle, and lay it aside to cool. It had a strangely mineral taste, but not unpleasant.

After a day or so, Jeremy began to get feverish and sick from the scalding he'd endured. He couldn't bear to eat or drink anything, and he hurt everywhere. He barely had the strength to stay awake, and when he slept, his dreams were terrible.

If he had continued that way, alone, he might not have survived much longer. But on the third day, he heard the sound of water falling over rocks, and vaguely realized he must be at the tip of the lake, at the place where the river flowed out of it. Malchouk's body was too large to go over the little waterfall, and ran aground in the shoals. Jeremy thought he saw movement on the path, and called out weakly.

He couldn't remember much about that part later, but he thought it wasn't long before he saw a pale face bent anxiously over his own. He felt strong hands lifting him into a boat, causing pain like fire to run all through his body, and after that he knew no more for a long time.

## Chapter Fifteen
### Lakkaia

He woke suddenly, and found himself in a comfortable bed for the first time in longer than he could remember. He was in a gray stone room, with the diffuse sunlight of the lake valley pouring in at the single window. There was no other person to be seen or heard.

Someone had removed most of his clothes, and put some kind of ointment on his burns. He felt much better, in fact, but he was awfully curious. He tried to move, and found himself still too weak for that. He had to be content with resting.

For a while, he was. And eventually, a short girl with dark hair entered the room and noticed that he was awake. She smiled.

"We thought you'd be waking soon," she said. Or something like that, anyway. She spoke the language of the Lachishites, but her accent was very strange and he didn't quite recognize some of the words she used. He returned the smile.

"Thank you for saving me," he told her, and he meant it sincerely.

"Ah, that was a little thing for us to do. You destroyed the Malchouk, and that was *everything*," she told him, with shining eyes. Jeremy thought about that for a minute.

"Then you are his goat herders?" he asked.

"We were. That, and his slaves and his dinner morsels," she agreed, with a look of hatred on her face.

"No one could ever defeat him, and those who tried were always killed and eaten. We had given up hope that we would ever be free of him, and we owe you a debt beyond hope of repayment," she went on.

"Thank the Most High, and not His humble servant," Jeremy replied automatically. She looked at him curiously, but made no answer to that.

Jeremy recovered quickly from his burns, and it wasn't long before he was hale and strong again. The

Malchikoi (for that was the name of those people) seemed in awe of him, and just as the Lachishites had done, at first they would gladly have made him both king and god, if he would have allowed it. But he gently corrected them, and taught them true knowledge, and they loved him all the more.

Jeremy spent not very long with these people, for they were only a few, and listened to him wide-eyed as children. They knew nothing of the world beyond the mist. The few of them who had ever climbed to the top of the valley remembered only that it was bitterly cold and painfully bright, and the rest of those people wanted no part of such a horrible place. It was hard for them to believe Jeremy had crossed so much of it.

He therefore said little to them about the lands far away, and kept his origins to himself. He was afraid if he told them too much about those things, it might make them curious enough to attempt the journey, and in that case such a traveller would likely die. If not the cold or wild beasts, then the *kronatsiya* plants or the priests of Cesme or the Sohrab slavers would get them. Jeremy preferred to let them live in peace.

After three months, therefore, Jeremy bid farewell to the Malchikoi, with many thanks.

Winter was growing old when he left the Lake of Fire, and he departed the valley by following the warm river that spilled out of the end of the lake. It was, in fact, the way he would have gone three months ago, if he hadn't been so foolish as to get captured by Malchouk.

The white mist dissipated soon after he left the vicinity of the lake, but the river still ran at the bottom of a deep valley. It was almost like a crack in the land, with sheer walls forty feet high, and the harsh winds on the tundra above passed right over it. There was a narrow strip of flat land on each side of the river, maybe thirty feet wide at the most, and in this narrow strip there were trees, such as Jeremy had not seen since leaving Cerise. There were larches and spruce and oak, with an occasional black willow tree weeping its yellow leaves into the stream. Some of the trees grew quite tall, until they reached the top of the valley walls. At that point the wind got them, and Jeremy saw more than one tall tree, perfect in every respect, except for a crazily wind-bitten top.

He saw no other people in all that land, though it was a pretty and fertile country. Perhaps the valley wasn't large enough to sustain a very big population for long, or maybe it was just that no one had ever explored the tundra thoroughly enough to find it.

Whatever the reason, Jeremy had the place all to himself.

Mixed with the woods he found little meadows of sedge and clover and other grasses, and occasional antelopes and wild cows grazing there. Jeremy had nothing to hunt with, and maybe it was just as well. . . herds could be dangerous if provoked. He caught fish from the river and gathered nuts and roots and things as he went along, to spare the dried food in his pack. It had to last him as long as possible.

It seemed that this place had never suffered from lack of rain, and Jeremy wondered if all of Rustrum would have looked this way, if not for King Joseph. That made him think of Jonah, and he wondered for a moment what his friend was doing that very day.

For a while, the valley had meandered almost due east, but gradually Jeremy noticed that it had curved around to the south instead. That concerned him at first because it seemed to be taking him back toward Rustrum; not at all the way he wanted to go. Indeed, he was beginning to wonder where the Most High was leading him, in the midst of all this desolate emptiness. Malchouk had been a nasty and vicious beast, but he was hardly the Great Enemy.

After many days, Jeremy began to encounter cultivated fields of wheat and barley scattered among the trees. By this time of year all the grain had been cut, leaving only brown stubble and a few stray stalks. He became much more cautious after that, for he didn't know if the people were friendly or not. He kept to the wooded sections of land near the river, where the thickest undergrowth and the heaviest shadows lay. The fields were deserted, but that was to be expected. It wasn't time for spring planting quite yet. As he went on, the signs of habitation grew steadily more numerous, and he began to pass scattered houses among the fields.

He debated whether to approach one of the houses and see if he could find out something about this new country. He had no weapons nor any good reason to explain himself, and he didn't want to be taken for a thief or an outlaw. Finally he chose one of the remotest cottages he had yet seen, and casually knocked on the door in the early morning.

A crack appeared in the door, and the eyes of an old woman looked out at him. Jeremy smiled.

"Lady, I am a stranger in these parts, and I have been without decent food for many days. If you would care to offer your hospitality this morning, I would be glad to repay you," he said, taking care to be especially courteous. The door opened a bit wider. She looked him up and down, then finally spoke.

"Would you now? Let's see the color of your coin first, my boy, and then we'll see what we can do," she said. This was not good manners, nor very friendly, but Jeremy overlooked it. He did have a little money with him, carried all the way from Rustrum and never used since then. He fished in his pack for a silver coin and offered it to the woman. He could have bought breakfast at any tavern with such a coin, and it was certainly valuable enough to satisfy a peasant woman. She looked at the coin, rubbed it, then deposited it somewhere in a pocket of her dress.

"Come around to the back," she ordered, and shut the door in his face before he had a chance to say anything. He shrugged and walked around to the other side of the cottage, where he found that another door opened into the kitchen. The old woman invited him to come in and sit at the rough wooden table while she busied herself about the stove.

He really was hungry, and it had been the simple truth that he'd not had a decent meal in several days, for trail rations and dried meat are hardly to be considered decent food. The kitchen was soon filled with the mouth-watering scent of frying bacon and eggs, which threatened to distract him from asking questions.

"Tell me, Lady, what is the name of this country I've come into?" he began pleasantly. She paused briefly at her cooking.

"Lakkaia," she replied shortly, getting back to work on the eggs as if there wasn't a second to lose. Her unfriendliness disappointed him, but he decided to try another tack.

"It's a beautiful country here. The people must be happy indeed, to live in such a place," he said. The woman turned and gave him a long look whose meaning he couldn't fathom, but she certainly didn't smile.

"Yes, I suppose so," she replied at last. She said it so dryly that he couldn't help getting the impression she meant exactly the opposite. But she turned back to the eggs with a firmness that indicated the subject was closed.

Jeremy had never encountered such a strange reaction from anyone before. He couldn't figure the woman out, and he'd about decided to have his breakfast and go try another house where the people might turn out to be nicer. He shut up and let her finish cooking. She placed a generous helping of bacon and eggs in front of him, with biscuits and fried potatoes and a glass of milk. He noted that apparently no one in Lakkaia worried about food supplies.

Before eating, he crossed his hands over his chest and thanked the Most High for the meal, and he always did.

"What are you doing?" the old woman asked, sharply. He looked up and saw a very strange expression on her face. . . a mixture of fear and something else he couldn't quite read. He was confused by her reaction, but he replied frankly.

"Lady, I wished to thank the Most High for His blessings on me this morning, and especially for this excellent meal," he said. The old woman seemed struck speechless.

"Stranger, take a word of advice. Never do that again, so long as you remain in Lakkaia," she whispered.

"But why not?" he asked, unable to think of any possible reason. The woman looked around swiftly, as if she might be about to say something. Then she apparently thought better of it.

"Never mind why not. If you don't know already, you'll find out soon enough," she warned. This interested Jeremy very much, but it was plain the old woman would not tell him anything more. He said nothing else to her while eating his breakfast, and when he was done he thanked her politely and went on his way. Her cold welcome and mysterious attitude puzzled him. But he had recognized the fear in her eyes when he prayed to the Most High, and that was the strangest thing of all. What could there be to fear in that?

Until he had more information he really had nothing on which to base even the flimsiest guess, so for now he decided not to speculate. As the old woman had said, he would find out soon enough.

Jeremy approached another house at mid afternoon and asked for directions. He was met with the same suspicious, unfriendly attitude the old woman had displayed. He began to think something was seriously wrong in this country, but the folk were so guarded and watchful that he could get nothing out of them. They all seemed to know something they didn't want to talk about. Or maybe dared not talk about. . . he couldn't tell.

Jeremy therefore asked no more questions, and went on his way without speaking to any of the people. He walked purposefully, as if he knew exactly where he was going and would not tolerate interference by anyone. He had found that this was usually the best way not to be thought suspicious, and even more importantly, not to be hindered. He abandoned his habit of moving quietly along the riverbank, and instead took to walking the roads.

These grew larger and more heavily used the farther south he went, until there was a regular highway. He still slipped into the woods to sleep, for tavern owners were notoriously gossipy and loose-tongued. That had always been the case in Rustrum, and he was willing to bet things were no different in Lakkaia. Certain things never changed.

He noticed a number of highly interesting things about that country as he went along, for there are many things one can see without needing to ask. The first thing, and one of the strangest, was that there seemed to be very few men about, and especially young ones. There seemed to be no particular shortage of young boys, but none above a certain age. There also seemed to be no lack of old men, and there was a normal variety of women of all ages. Jeremy was very much alone in his age group. The few young men he did see were sickly, or crippled, or some other such thing.

The other thing he noticed by and by was the lack of open churches. There were many church *buildings*, to be sure, and he only gradually realized that none of them were being used. In all of Lakkaia, he encountered not a single functioning church. Nor did he ever see a priest, nor even an ordinary person praying. That disturbed him.

From the lack of men, he suspected that some sort of military operation was going on, or about to go on. The tight-lipped Lakkaians never seemed to discuss it, even amongst themselves, unless it were in private. Jeremy was finally driven to the point of eavesdropping on conversations in restaurants. He wasted countless hours in such places, listening to the same foolish gossip retold in longer and shorter forms about a hundred different people he'd never heard of. Only very rarely did he manage to glean a stray comment that was of any use to him. He heard two women on different days mention that their husbands had gone to "the City", wherever that was. He could have sworn he overheard another one say something about an enemy in the south, and that interested him exceedingly, but he never heard this repeated.

Jeremy was unbearably frustrated by all these hints and oblique comments. He wished many times for his messenger boys, for they had always kept him well informed of even the faintest rumor in Cerise. Here, he felt constantly in the dark about things everyone else took for granted. He finally decided, for lack of any better plan, to head for "the City" himself. That seemed to be where things were happening.

He didn't have a difficult time finding his way, for there was only a single major road that ran through Lakkaia from end to end. The land was thickly populated, with almost every square inch of it either farmed or used for some other purpose. There was little empty space, and the farther he walked the less of it he saw.

And yet. . . when he came to the city of Lakkaia itself, he found that it surpassed anything he could possibly have imagined. It was built on a large island in the middle of the river, but it had long since spilled over onto both banks as well. The city was so large that when Jeremy came to the northern edge of it, he couldn't see the far side. It went on for miles. . . street after street, building after building, crowded and throbbing with people; such throngs as Jeremy had never before seen or imagined. He stood in awe.

The city had no wall, being far too large for that, he supposed. It lay open and unguarded for all he could tell. Far away, at the very edge of sight, there rose a tall gray tower that overlooked all else. Jeremy could not have said why, but he felt the tower had an evil air, even from this distance. He decided to avoid that place, at least for now. But where should he go?

The city stretched ahead of him in all directions, filling the entire valley. He could see what looked like greenstuff of some kind growing thickly on the flat rooftops, but he couldn't tell what it might be. Almost all the buildings seemed to be the same height, and squeezed very close together. There were no other interesting features to be seen.

Since he had no particular destination in mind, Jeremy set off walking in a straight line towards what he guessed to be the center of the city. He was fairly correct in this, as you will see, but he would have done better to go elsewhere.

## Chapter Sixteen
## The Great City

Jeremy walked all day long through the immense city. It felt cramped and ill-designed in comparison with Cerise or even Rustrum, for the streets were so narrow and the crowds so thick that he constantly had to elbow his way among the people. At first he tried to excuse himself when he had to jostle someone, until he noticed that no one else bothered to say anything at such times. Then he stopped, because he thought it unwise to draw attention to himself. None of the people smiled or even met his eyes, looking down only at the paving stones as they made their way to wherever it was they were going.

The buildings were butted right up against each other with no space in between, and with very few exceptions almost every single one was exactly the same height- four stories high. They were all made of red brick, with few windows. He knew there had to be a reason for so much sameness, but he could only guess what it might be. The only differences he saw were minor ones. Some of the buildings had wooden awnings on the front that extended out a short distance over the street, and sometimes there were steps leading up (or down) to the front doors. People were constantly coming in and out of these places, and he toyed with the idea of going into one of them himself to see what might be inside. Then he thought better of it. Walking into a place uninvited could cause trouble.

It was also strangely warm for a day in late winter, but Jeremy paid little attention to that until later.

It took quite a long time to make much progress through the city. After several hours he still didn't seem much closer to the center than he had when he started. He began to worry that all the people on the street would eventually go home and leave him alone on the streets to be picked up as a vagrant by the town watch, if they had such a thing. He'd seen nothing resembling an inn the entire time he'd been in the city. Yet surely they had visitors from time to time?

There had been inns in the smaller villages he'd seen in Lakkaia, so why not here?

It crossed his mind that he might possibly have passed several inns without realizing it, since none of the buildings were marked in any way. Another annoying example of everyone seeming to know everything already.

After a while, he began to get tired and thirsty. He wondered (a little sourly) if anyone would tell him where to get a drink of water.

Late in the afternoon, when the dusk was just beginning to gather over the city, a trumpet blast was heard to echo down Jeremy's street. This seemed to put the crowd into the greatest confusion imaginable. Everyone jostled and scraped even more than usual, pressing up against the walls of the buildings on both sides so as to leave a narrow opening down the middle of the street. Jeremy was almost crushed between a fat man in front of him and the brick wall behind. He was completely walled in with people and couldn't budge an inch to either side. He was afraid the man would suffocate him if he didn't move soon.

One of the wooden awnings hung just above him, and Jeremy noticed that it had an iron crossbar bolted into the side of the building to support it. He reached up and grabbed hold of the crossbar and pulled himself up above the crowd. There was room enough for him to sit there on the edge of the awning, and it seemed to be strong enough to bear his weight. He sat there breathing deeply and relishing the open space. The place where he'd been standing against the building immediately closed up when he left it, and he couldn't have gotten back down on the street even if he'd wanted to.

Soon, a group of soldiers approached from down the street, and as they came closer he saw that they were escorting a litter carried by six strong men. Upon it reclined a man, and the crowd was utterly silent as he passed by. There was no cheering or waving, as there might have been in Rustrum at such a time. Every head was bowed, as if no one dared look at the man. Jeremy did likewise, but his position on the awning meant he could still see fairly well anyway.

The litter proceeded slowly down the street, for no matter how tightly the people pressed up against the walls, there was still very little room for it to pass.

Presently the procession reached the spot where Jeremy perched. The soldiers were dressed all in silver and black, and carried wicked-looking curved blades at their sides. But the man himself, when he came into view, was much more interesting than any of his soldiers had been.

He wore a cape of blue silk, edged with black fur of some kind. The blue had unmistakably come from Cerise. Jeremy hadn't known dye was traded in such distant parts. He had a moment of idle curiosity about how long it must have taken to reach Lakkaia and how incredibly much it must have cost after such a journey.

The man had black hair, grown down to his shoulders, and in his hand he held something like a sceptre or a mace; it was hard to tell which. He had a proud, cruel face which made you think he had done terrible things. It gave the impression that he smiled often. . . and that men had died when he did so. Jeremy shivered.

Just as the litter was passing, the man sat up abruptly.

"Stop!" he cried in a harsh voice that made even some of his soldiers flinch. The procession halted immediately. The man looked around as if searching for something, then raised his mace (for that was what it was) and pointed directly at Jeremy.

"There he is! Bring him here immediately!" the man ordered. The soldiers jumped to obey him, and the ordinary city folk stumbled and trampled each other in their haste to get out of the way. Anyone who wasn't quick enough, the soldiers slashed or kicked aside.

Jeremy didn't know what was going on, but he quickly decided it probably wouldn't be healthy to go along quietly.   The man had not looked like a welcoming friend, and the soldiers themselves were coming after him with swords drawn.

There was no way to escape into the street. The crowd was so thick, he could never move fast enough to get away.   That left above.   The awning didn't extend very far along the building, but there were windows above it that he thought he could reach.

Jeremy wasted no more time.   He stood up on the end of the awning and reached up to the sill of the window above him.   It was just barely within reach.   He clung tightly and hoisted himself up, punching through the oiled paper that covered the opening.   He thanked the Most High it hadn't been glass.

He hadn't seen any of the soldiers with bows or spears, and apparently his impression was correct.   No one threw or fired anything at him, at least.   He scrambled over the sill and tumbled into a room too dark for his eyes to see what it contained just yet.   He heard shouts from outside and the sound of someone trying to climb the awning to come after him. Doubtless others would be entering the building by the front door and coming up the stairs, but that would take longer.

He blindly fled toward where he imagined the door would be, with both arms held out ahead of him to keep from running full force into a wall or some other obstacle. He kicked against something sharp with his left foot and felt it cut through his boot. The pain was enough to make him hobble, but he dared not slow down to look at the wound.

His eyes soon began to adjust to the dimness a little bit, and he found the door on the opposite wall. He yanked it open and found himself on a balcony of sorts, three floors high above a courtyard. He could look down and see soldiers running into the building from where the front door must be, directly below him. Unfortunately, that also meant they could see him too. He dropped instantly to a low crouch to make himself less conspicuous, but it was too late. One of the soldiers gave a shout and pointed at the balcony. Therefore he gave up the idea of concealment and ran as fast as he could towards the stairs at the end of the balcony. He was helped by the fact that the soldiers would have to climb two flights of stairs and circle the almost the entire balcony twice before they could reach his position.

When he got to the foot of the stairs, he climbed quickly to the next level, and then the next. He was staying ahead of the soldiers, for now, but he was beginning to get winded and he knew he was going to have to find a place to hide soon or they would catch him.

He burst onto the roof, finding it (to his astonishment) entirely covered by a grape vineyard. He had no time to marvel at this, however, for the soldiers could not be far behind him. He plunged headlong into the grapes, aiming as nearly as he could judge for the back edge of the building. The vines grew on tall screens higher than his head, and he thanked the Most High for the protection they gave him.

He reached the back of the building without incident, and eeled over the low wall separating it from the next structure. If he hadn't known better, he might have thought he was somewhere far out in the middle of farmland, for he found himself slipping from a grape vineyard into a bean field. This wasn't quite so good for concealment, but Jeremy hunched over and scrabbled along on all fours, taking care to keep his body below the level of the beans.

He crossed several rooftops in this way, passing from the bean field through several others, until the place where he'd seen the cruel man was far behind him.  He took refuge at last in a corn field, thickly shrouded from view by the green stalks.

He knew this was only a temporary safety, for he'd have to go down into the city again eventually. The city folk must work these rooftop fields, too, and he would always be in danger of being discovered by one of them.  In the meantime, though, the corn field would have to do.  He was too exhausted, and his foot hurt too much to go on.

Now that he had time to think about it, he wondered very much how it was possible for crops to be growing in the middle of the winter.  The fields outside the city had been lying empty, ready for planting when the frost was past.  Yet here, on the rooftops, there were green things growing in profusion, as if it were late summer.  He had no clue how to explain the fact, so he let it drop for now.  There would be time to figure it out later.  He had more urgent things to think about right now.

His left foot was throbbing with pain, and he noticed it all the more since he wasn't having to run for his life.  His boot was sliced open and caked with blood.  He gingerly removed it from his foot, discovering a deep gash between his big toe and his other toes.  It was almost three inches long, and still seeping blood.  Jeremy winced, not entirely from pain.

A bad foot would slow him down, and that could be deadly.

He crept quietly through the field until he came to a water pump, and there he cleaned the wound as thoroughly as he could. The water was icy cold, and numbed his skin. That was good, because it meant what he had to do next wouldn't hurt quite so much. He let the water run over his foot for a good long time. Then he opened his pack and took out his bottle of salt. He took a deep breath to gather his courage before rubbing a handful of it into the cut. Salt was the only thing he had with him to prevent infection. He had to clench his teeth to keep from screaming; the pain was so intense it almost made him throw up. He had nothing to wrap the foot with except a strip torn from one of the extra shirts in his pack. He hoped that would do.

After all this, he returned to the most secluded part of the corn field that he could find, next to where a brick chimney rose out of the ground and provided some warmth. He dared not build a fire, so the next best thing was to take advantage of one built in the building below him. The chimney was much too hot to lie next to, but there was a quite comfortable zone within a few feet of it.

He lay down on the dirt, resting his head against his pack. The pain in his foot kept him from sleeping right away, so he looked up at the stars that were just beginning to twinkle in the dusky sky and thought for a while. He felt quite sure there was something in this place he was meant to do, and the more he thought about it the more certain he was that it had something to do with the man he'd seen earlier, and the tall building at the center of the city.

The thing that concerned him most was why the man had sent the soldiers after him. Jeremy had certainly never seen him before, nor been anywhere near Lakkaia. Yet the man had seemed to recognize him. He'd said "there he is", as if he'd been looking for Jeremy in particular. Why should that be? Jeremy had done nothing (that he knew of) to offend or injure anybody in Lakkaia.

Of course it was true that he might be in trouble *now*, since he'd run from the soldiers and all. But that didn't explain what they'd wanted with him in the first place.

He wondered at first if they'd mistaken him for someone else. Surely not, though. His fiery red hair made him unlikely to be taken for anyone but himself. Or maybe it had something to do with his age. . . maybe they thought he'd run away from the army or something. He even started to wonder if the old woman who'd fed him breakfast on the first day he came to Lakkaia might have reported him as a dangerous outlaw.

Try as he might, Jeremy couldn't figure out what to make of it all. Deep in his heart, he also wondered if he might at long last be getting close to the Great Enemy. That idea scared him more than he liked to admit. He was devoted to the purpose for which the Most High had sent him, but that didn't mean he was eager for a fight.

## Chapter Seventeen
### Maia

Jeremy woke in the morning to find a girl looking down at him. He was startled and sat up quickly, reaching for his dagger without thinking, before he remembered he didn't have one anymore.

She was not much younger than he was, and looked neither friendly nor unfriendly. . . just curious. She stepped back a few paces when he sat up. She was carrying a bucket and seemed to have come to pick corn; there were a few ears trailing silk tassels over the lip of the bucket. Her long hair was the same dark yellow as the corn silk, and she wore a long brown dress with gray fur at the hems. All this he noticed in an instant, without thinking. And then he couldn't help looking at her a while longer, for she was without exception the most beautiful girl he had ever seen. The first thing that came to his mind was what a dazzling smile she must have. She wasn't smiling now, though. She was looking at him very solemnly.

"Have you run away?" she asked, getting right to the point. Jeremy wasn't sure what she was talking about, but that didn't make any difference, since she had apparently made up her mind already before he answered.

"You know what they'll do when they find you," she continued, nodding mysteriously. He didn't know, and he was afraid to guess. He quickly decided he'd better get over his calf-eyed staring and be perfectly straightforward with the girl. She was the most sympathetic person he'd met ever since he came to Lakkaia.

"I'm a stranger in this land, I'm afraid," he told her. Her eyes widened a bit.

"Then you're not in the army?" she asked.

"No. But yesterday a group of soldiers chased me here for no reason that I could tell, because a man with black hair and a blue cape ordered them to," he said. She thought about this for some time.

"That must have been the Vizier. He's the only man in the city who wears a blue cape," she said, half to herself. The bucket of corn was momentarily forgotten.

"The Vizier is a bad enemy to have, stranger. It's a good thing you ran away, for he would have had your head on a spike before another hour had passed, if he'd caught you," she told him gravely. Jeremy felt a little sick.

"But why?" he asked. The girl shrugged.

"The Vizier knows things. Some people say he's a sorcerer, or even a demon. If he wished, he could listen to this conversation we're having right now," she told him.

"That doesn't scare you?" he asked, intrigued. She laughed at that.

"Oh, stranger, what a silly thought! You really don't know much, do you?" she asked, still smiling. He couldn't help noticing that her smile was just as dazzling as he'd thought it would be, but he firmly put that thought out of his mind.

"Tell me, then," he suggested. She seemed to consider it.

"It would be a long tale, stranger, and the corn needs picking. But if you care to help me with that afterwards, I'll gladly tell you all about the Vizier. You may not live long, if I don't," she said in a softer voice. She took the ears of corn out of her bucket, upended it on the ground, and sat down on it.

"My name is Maia, and I am the youngest daughter of the Master of the Tenth Ward, which is this part of the city we're in right now. For a long time, the King ruled our land fairly and generously, and my father was his dearest friend on the council. But we began to have troubles with invaders from the south, and the people had lived in peace for so long that we were not prepared to fight them. They ravaged the land between here and the mountains, and even the city itself was in danger of being destroyed. Then the Vizier appeared one morning, none knew from where, and offered to save us from the invaders, if the King would give him whatever reward he should ask for, after it was done. The King was in desperation, for the invaders were pouring through the very gates of the city, and he made an oath to give whatever the Vizier should ask, if he could deliver us. Therefore the Vizier took command of the city, and he went himself to the forefront of the battle, and it is said that he spoke in an unknown tongue, and cracks full of raging flame opened in the earth and devoured most of the invaders, and the rest fled in terror. The Vizier returned in triumph to the King, and demanded that he should be made permanent viceroy and regent of the kingdom. The King had sworn, and could not refuse him. Since then, the Vizier has been the real power in all of Lakkaia. He has the King under his thumb, and anyone else who opposes him soon finds himself with his head on a spike atop the fortress. He is a cruel man," the girl said.

"Yet you don't fear him?" Jeremy asked again.

"No, not really. I can do him no harm, therefore he cares nothing about what I may say or do. I've told you nothing which isn't known by every child in Lakkaia, so what then should I fear?" she asked. It seemed reasonable, but Jeremy wondered if she was really correct about that. The Vizier seemed the sort of man who might lop someone's head off just for the fun of it, if he ever had a moment of boredom.

"In any case, the people may fear him, but they know at least we are safe from destruction. Now, the Vizier is leading a great muster of all the men in the kingdom, for he means to lead the army across the southern mountains and destroy forever the invaders who attacked us before. He says they are in a time of weakness, and now is the moment when we must strike and crush them, so they will never be a danger to us again," the girl went on.

"Is that why you thought I'd run away?" Jeremy asked.

"Yes, for all the young men are gathered on the fields south of the city, except those unfit for fighting. The Vizier says the attack must begin soon, but only he knows exactly when," she said. Jeremy digested this.

"There's another thing that interests me, Maia," he told her.

"Yes?" she asked, with another pretty smile.

"Was it the Vizier who closed the Houses of the Most High?" he asked bluntly. Maia's smile faded.

"Yes. . . he says that the people should not listen to superstitious nonsense like that anymore, and that all it did for us before was to make us weak and soft. Some of the people opposed him then, but after a thousand new heads sat atop the fortress walls, he had his way. The Houses were closed, the priests killed or banished to the far edges of the kingdom, and discussion of that subject was forbidden in public, on pain of death," she said. Jeremy was horrified.

"And the people allowed this to go on?" he asked, not willing to believe it.

"Some of the people agreed with him, and many more have joined him since then. Those who still believe in the old ways are few and far between, nowadays. No one can say for sure, but in all of

Lakkaia there are probably no more than a handful," she told him.

"And the others?" he whispered.

"Killed or fled into the wilds," she answered simply. "The Vizier tells us that some of those who fled have joined our enemies and will keep trying to destroy us as long as any of them are still alive."

Jeremy didn't know what to say.

"And what do you believe, Maia?" he asked. She studied him briefly, as if sizing him up.

"I could ask you the same question, stranger. I guess by your questions what you think, but these are dangerous times, and I just finished telling you what can happen to believers in the old ways in Lakkaia," she answered. This was a fair enough challenge.

"My name is Jeremy, and I am a prophet of the Most High. And if what you have told me of the Vizier is true, then I am his sworn enemy unless he repents, and I cannot rest until all his power in Lakkaia is destroyed," he declared boldly.

"Strong words, Jeremy," she said, looking at him in a new light. He shrugged, and she seemed to make a decision.

"Then I will tell you that my family is among the last of the old believers in Lakkaia, and you should be very thankful it was I who found you in the corn this morning. Otherwise. . ." she didn't need to finish the thought; he knew what she was suggesting.

"Come," she said, "we've talked a long time, and the corn won't pick itself. You owe me some help this morning."

Jeremy stood up, being careful not to put any weight on his injured foot, and helped Maia fill the bucket with ears of corn. When it was full she took it to a bin near the water pump and returned with an empty bucket for Jeremy also.

"Maia, how is it that all this grows in the middle of the winter?" he asked.

"The Vizier says it isn't wise to let our food supply depend on the outside so much. The city is so large, it could starve quickly if there was ever a siege again. So he put forth his power over the city, to make it always warm. It only reaches as high as the plants grow, though. If you jumped high enough, or if you went on top of one of the taller buildings, you'd be back out in the cold air," she explained.

Jeremy was tempted to give this a try, but then he remembered his foot and thought better of it. The pain of landing again after a jump wasn't worth satisfying his curiosity.

Maia wasn't a chatty person, for she didn't talk much while they picked the corn. He kept stealing glances at her while they worked, but she seemed not to notice. About noon, they reached a point that seemed to satisfy her for awhile.

"Well!" she declared, "What would you say to something to eat?" Jeremy agreed it was high time for a meal of some sort. She walked briskly toward the water pump, and looked back when she noticed him lagging behind.

"What's wrong with your foot?" she asked, as if noticing it for the first time. Come to think of it, she might not have noticed earlier, because picking the corn didn't make him have to walk much.

"I cut it on something yesterday. It hurts to walk much," he admitted. She came back to where he stood.

"Can I see?" she asked. Jeremy thought it was probably a good idea to look at the cut again himself by now, so he sat down on the ground and began to gingerly unwrap the cloth bandage. It hurt a little to take it off and the foot started to trickle blood again. He was relieved to see there wasn't any sign of infection yet. Hopefully the salt had done its job.

However pleased Jeremy might have been, Maia was horrified.

"Jeremy, that's terrible! Why didn't you tell me before you picked corn all morning?" she asked. He started to answer, but she went on as if she'd never asked.

"You need to get a proper bandage on that immediately, before you lose your foot. I'll take you downstairs and have Mother do it at once," she decided. He wondered wryly where she'd learned to have such a take-charge attitude. He didn't disagree with her about what needed to be done, but he did like to be asked what he thought. Still, no need to start a quarrel just to make a point.

"Alright," he agreed. Instead of trying to rewrap the foot in the old bandage, Jeremy leaned against Maia and hobbled on one foot to the head of the stairs. At that point she couldn't help him very well anymore, and he had to sit down on the top step and slide down one at a time.

Maia's apartment took up the entire top floor of the building. Part of it was given over to storage and office space for the Tenth Ward, but most of it was living quarters for the Master's rather large family. Maia was the youngest child of the Master himself, but all of her six brothers still lived at home, along with their wives and children, and even a few aunts and cousins and assorted other relations. Altogether, thirty-six people lived in the Master's household. The apartment was large enough that no one had to feel crowded, but Jeremy gathered that most other people in the city were not so fortunate.

Maia's mother was in the kitchen when they came in, slicing potatoes on a large board with two other women. She looked up from her work and came to see who her daughter had brought home, wiping potato juice on her apron as she crossed the room. She was a lady with silver hair and a kind face, and Jeremy liked her immediately.

"And who might this be, Maia?" she asked.

"This is Jeremy, a stranger in the city, and he needs your help. He has an injured foot," Maia blurted breathlessly.

"Let me see your foot, boy," she said, kneeling down to examine it more easily.

"That's a nasty cut," she commented, "but we'll have it fixed up soon enough. Come sit down in the parlor." The parlor was next to the kitchen, and Jeremy sat down on a soft chair to wait. Maia's mother went to fetch whatever items she needed for her doctoring, while Maia herself sat in another chair to wait for her.

"Mother is very good at this sort of thing, so you mustn't worry at all," Maia promised him.

"Alright, I won't worry then," he said, and then smiled. It was nice to be among friends again.

Maia's mother returned with a clean bandage, a pan of water, and some sweet-smelling salve. She washed the foot expertly, applied a generous amount of salve, and wrapped the bandage snugly but not too tight. Jeremy felt much better, and thanked her very much.

"Now, child, of course you'll stay with us a few days until you've recovered a bit, and then we'll see what needs to be done to get you back on your way. I'm afraid Lakkaia is not the most hospitable of places these days," she said regretfully.

Jeremy couldn't accept such hospitality without telling her everything. She listened carefully, without interrupting.

"This house has not forgotten the Most High, and will not, so long as I am mistress here. None of our family will say anything about you beyond these walls, and I judge the Vizier is too occupied with his preparations for war to spare much time or energy searching for you. If it turns out otherwise. . . well, there are certain risks that one must take regardless of the danger involved," she said.

"Thank you," Jeremy said.

"Thank the Most High," she replied. She gathered all her materials together to put them back wherever she had gotten them, and stood up.

"Now, say nothing more about it, and Maia will find you a place to sleep," she said.

Maia led him out of the parlor and down a short hall until she came to the last door on the right.

"This room belongs to my brother Marcus. He's not married yet, and not often here. The Vizier doesn't allow anyone with imperfections to serve in the army, but he does make everyone work to support it. Marcus is a bladesmith, and they keep him very busy lately. If he does by chance come home, he won't mind sharing," Maia told him.

Marcus' room was not large, being about the same size as Jeremy's office in Cerise, but it was neat and clean. There was a bed against the wall that looked as if it were rarely slept in, and a few books on a shelf. A wooden chest sat at the foot of the bed, and there was a lamp on a table near the head. On the table sat a worn copy of the Book of the Prophets, the first one Jeremy had seen since leaving his own copy with Daniel in Kalavah. Maia noticed his glance.

"Marcus has another copy to keep with him. That's an old one he only uses when he's home sometimes," she said.

"I gave my copy to a brave man who was teaching the barbarians in the mountains," Jeremy murmured.

"Oh, but you should have said so! I'll make sure you get another one before you leave us," Maia promised him.

### Chapter Eighteen
### The Gap

Jeremy stayed almost three weeks with Maia's family. Winter dragged on in the country outside, but summer reigned forever in the city. When his foot had healed somewhat, Maia took him to a taller building next door and led him up into the freezing cold air beyond the Bubble, as they called it. The building was only one floor taller than all the others, and it was incredible to stand there on the icy roof amid the freezing wind, yet look down just below on green fields of wheat and corn drowsing in the warmth of a summer afternoon. He could only look on in speechless amazement.

It didn't take long for him to have his fill of gazing, though. The wind was too cold up there to enjoy it for long. Maia laughed at his amazement. She, who had never known cold for more than an hour in her life, couldn't understand why Jeremy found the lack of it so amazing. He loved the sound of her laughter, and wondered if he would ever hear a laugh like that again. When he stopped to think about it, he couldn't have said what was so different about her; just that he had never met anyone so merry and wise, nor anyone whose company made him so happy. She had two jobs she had to do, and since both of them were solitary kinds of things, Jeremy was able to go with her to both of them. One was picking corn and beans, and otherwise tending the plants on the roof. The other was carving bows and arrows from ash wood for the army. She turned out to be quite an expert archer. Jeremy had learned how to use a sword while he was a page, but he'd never picked up a bow. Maia tried to teach him, sitting on the roof and aiming at a chimney or a bucket. She had the cool and practiced aim of someone who never missed a target, but this was one thing Jeremy never learned to do. She tried not to laugh at him, but when she did, he couldn't say he really minded.

When he was quite well, Jeremy reluctantly began to think of moving on. He didn't wish to impose any more than necessary on the hospitality of these good people, especially since he knew that his presence in their house brought them into danger.

Therefore he went to Maia's father, the Master of the Ward, and declared his purpose.

"If you go now, you may find little to hinder you in the city. The Vizier and the army have departed this very morning towards the southern mountains, and they will not return for many months. You may, with a little luck, slip out of the city unrecognized, and if you take some other direction so as not to catch up to the army, you should do well," the Master said.

"Sir, what lies beyond those mountains?" he asked, for he had long thought that they had a nagging familiarity he couldn't quite dismiss.

"No one knows for certain," the Master said. "The traders who come now and again say that beyond the mountains there are hills, and a broad plain atop a high cliff, and beyond that a desert and a sea. But we have no maps beyond the passes through the mountains. The Vizier alone knows that country well, for some say he came from there in his youth. He colors his robes with the blue dye of that land, which he pays dearly for the traders to bring him. He says, in fact, that the source of that dye is one of the things we shall capture during the great war, and then it will make us rich, in payment for the terrible injuries those wicked people did us when they invaded our land."

Jeremy immediately recognized that the Master could only be talking about the land of Rustrum, and he was filled with fear. King Joseph had been wicked, but Jeremy knew quite well that he had never had strength or courage enough to invade Lakkaia. The people of Rustrum knew nothing of what lay beyond the mountains. Therefore the Vizier was lying, for his own evil purposes.

And yet he might very well succeed in his plans, for the army of Lakkaia was immense, and would burst upon Jonah unprepared. They could march unnoticed across the High Plain, and sweep down to capture Cerise before anyone was even aware of their approach. With that done, a flood of enemies could overrun all the valley land until Rustrum was surrounded without hope. Jonah would do the best he could, but after a bitter struggle the city would certainly be destroyed. Some might escape by sea, perhaps, but the land itself would be laid waste, plundered and burned to nothing. Jeremy could see nothing to prevent it, for he could never hope to outrun the army, nor to cross the passes without being captured or killed. He could spend weeks (at least) journeying back to the east and crossing through the land of the Lachishites. All this passed through his mind in seconds.

"Master, the people beyond the mountains are not the ones who attacked Lakkaia. I don't know who those people might have been, but the Vizier is lying. The king of the people beyond the mountains is a righteous man, and this invasion would be a terrible wickedness," Jeremy declared. The Master looked sad.

"That may be, but will you convince the army not to follow him? I think not," he said. Jeremy didn't doubt the truth of that.

"Then I must warn the King of Rustrum before it's too late," he said grimly.

"That's impossible. The army will fill every pass in the mountains for days, and you would never get across," the Master said firmly.

"Then there must be another way to get through the mountains," Jeremy insisted.

"There is no other way. There are only the three passes, and you don't have time to search for another. The river of Lakkaia passes through the mountains in a deep gorge full of rushing water and knives of stone, but none have ever gone that way and lived to tell the tale," the Master said, shaking his head. Jeremy didn't hesitate a second.

"Then I will take the river," he said firmly.

"Are you mad?" the Master gasped in horror.

"Not at all," Jeremy assured him, though he was deathly afraid of what he planned to do.

The Master could not restrain him, so he provided Jeremy with rich clothes and food for a long journey, and money enough to buy a sturdy boat. Maia wept when he departed, and that almost cracked his courage, but he was determined not to give up.

"Maia, will you come with me to the head of the gorge? No farther than that, but I may need your help to survive the journey," he asked diffidently. He was shy about asking her, but he knew no one else he could trust. She stopped crying and agreed immediately. Jeremy looked at the Master and his wife.

"Sir and Lady, she will be back in the city no later than three days hence, if you allow her to go," he promised. He could tell that the Master hesitated, but after some obvious deep thought he reluctantly agreed.

They walked quickly to the nearest part of the city next to the river, and there Jeremy purchased both a sturdy wooden boat, a barrel full of apples, and a hammer and nails.

"What's all that for?" Maia asked as she helped him load it into the boat.

"You'll see," he told her.

The river was swift, and the current carried the boat far from the city within hours. The head of the gorge was about forty miles south of the city, a trip that required not quite eight hours to finish. When the walls of the mountains began to rise up in the late afternoon sunlight, Jeremy paddled the boat to the east bank and dragged it up onto a sandy beach. The sound of the Gap could be heard clearly, not that far away.

"Now what?" Maia asked him, crossing her arms.

"Watch," he told her. He took the hammer and pried the lid off the apple barrel, then unceremoniously kicked it over and dumped the fruit on the ground.

"What did you do that for?" she wanted to know. He waved a hand to shush her while he upended the barrel and emptied it of the remaining apples. They made a little pile of red and gold on the beach, and he picked one up to take a bite of it as he finished his work.

He set the barrel back on its bottom end.

"Alright, Maia, let's gather some hay and leaves and whatever things like that we can find. But nothing sharp or hard," he cautioned her. She began to get an idea of what he had in mind, and she didn't like it much.

"You're crazy, Jeremy. You'll be beaten to death inside that barrel, or smashed against a rock and drowned. You have no idea how bad the Gap is," she told him.

"No, but neither do you, really. No one's ever come back to say what it was like, after all," he reminded her. He was trying to be light-hearted, but he could tell the effort wasn't working. He took a more serious tone.

"Maia, I know the danger. But the Most High will protect me. Don't worry," he told her, putting a hand on her arm. She said nothing to this, but she did start to gather hay.

Soon they had gathered a large pile of dry grass and leaves, and Jeremy climbed into the barrel. It smelled sweetly of apples inside. He pulled his pack inside after him, putting it next to his belly and curling around it. Then he and Maia carefully stuffed as much of the empty space as they could with hay and leaves to keep him from being bruised and battered quite so much.

At the last, when the lid was ready to be put on, he smiled up at her.

"Don't worry, Maia. I'll be fine," he promised her. She didn't look as if she believed it. She bent down and kissed him quickly, and before he had time even to think what to say, she had the lid in place. He touched his lips with one hand, wonderingly.

It was pitch dark inside the barrel, and the echoes were loud as Maia nailed the lid in place. If it came off while he was in the water, it would probably mean almost certain death.

At last it was done, and Maia pushed the barrel over so she could roll it down to the water. Rolling over and over down the beach made him a little dizzy, giving him a grim foretaste of what he was in for. He knew the Gap itself would be a thousand times worse. He said a prayer to the Most High to be with him.

He felt the barrel roll into the river, and Maia gave it a last shove out into the main current. He wondered if she stood on the beach and watched until he floated out of sight. She had a long, cold journey back to the city.

For a while, the barrel floated fairly smoothly. It settled down in such a way that Jeremy's back was on the bottom side, with his pack resting on his stomach. There were no leaks (yet) that he could tell. Just warm, apple-scented darkness, and the muffled gurgle of water from outside the barrel. He could hear little else, and he was actually glad he couldn't see.

Then, with horrible suddenness, the barrel plunged down and spun over, smacking Jeremy's head against the wood. The water picked up speed, and he could hear it roaring even through the barrel walls. He was rolled and spun and twisted crazily, in a way that would nauseate even the most iron stomach. His heart was in his mouth with terror, but that was nothing compared to what was coming. With a sickening crunch the barrel smashed into a rock, slamming his face into wood and bloodying his nose. No sooner was that done than he hit another rock and smashed his ear so hard he saw stars.

Jeremy remembered the rest of that journey only in bits and pieces. He was constantly battered and smashed against the barrel walls, getting bruised and bloody and dazed with pain, in spite of the hay. At one point he vomited, though he couldn't remember it afterward. After a while, he began to notice water swishing around inside, and he decided solemnly that the barrel must have sprung a leak. He knew, in a confused kind of way, that this meant he would eventually sink, but he was too sick and hurting to care.

After what seemed forever, the gorge opened out again and the river gradually calmed down to its ordinary placid self. It took Jeremy a while to comprehend that the horrible ride was over, and he was too weak by then to do anything about it.

In reality, Jeremy's headlong ride through the Gap had taken less than four hours, and it was now night in the world outside. No one noticed the barrel as it floated downstream for the rest of the night. Jeremy dozed in a fitful kind of way, too sick and hungry and thirsty to really sleep.

If he'd been able to see, he might have thought the countryside along the river looked strangely familiar, and as he floated ever onward, more and more so. The river continued to get broader and shallower, and the hills less steep and more rounded, until near morning the bottom of the barrel scraped against gravel, and came to rest on a sand bar where the river made a sharp turn to the west around an outcrop of stone.

Jeremy woke slightly when the barrel ran aground, but he didn't have the strength to kick the lid off and escape. Instead, the stillness soon lulled him into a deeper sleep.

### *Chapter Nineteen*
### *Melech*

A few hours later, when the light of early morning came streaming across the valley, Jeremy was wakened by the sound of voices. They were muffled through the barrel, but he could make out what they said.

"Do you think there might be something inside, Papa?" the first voice said.

"Maybe. It floats low in the water for an empty, but it might just be leaky," another voice answered. Jeremy tried to shout, but all that came out was a low groan no one outside the barrel could possibly have heard.

Soon he felt the barrel being dragged farther up onto the bar away from the water's edge.

"It's definitely got something in it, Papa. It's way too heavy," the first voice panted from just outside. He was evidently the one dragging the barrel.

"Well, run home and fetch a hammer then, and we'll see," the father told him.

There followed a lengthy pause when nothing else happened. Jeremy couldn't tell if both the men had gone to fetch the hammer, or if the father was still on the sand bar waiting for the son to come back.

Whichever it was, he eventually felt the barrel being stood upright, and heard the squeal of nails pulling out of wood. The lid came free with a wet pop, and sunlight poured in on Jeremy's head.

"Papa, there's a man in here!" the younger man cried out.

"Is he dead?" the father demanded.

"I don't- " the son began, but just then Jeremy exerted all his strength and groaned again, loud enough that there was no mistaking the sound.

"He's alive!" the man cried. Jeremy felt the barrel laid down again, and strong hands grabbed him under the armpits and hauled him out onto the sand bar. He must have made a terrible sight, covered in blood and vomit and bruised and scraped all over.

Then he heard the very last sound he would have expected.

*"Jeremy?"* the young man said, in disbelief. There is no mistaking the sound of utter astonishment in a human voice, and this one was full of it. The man splashed water in his face and washed away the blood and vomit.

"Papa, look!" the man cried. There was a great deal of commotion then, as the two men argued over him.

"Papa, look at him! Look at his hair and his face. Could there be two like that? I tell you, it's Jeremy," the young man said.

"But that's impossible!" the father insisted. With an effort, Jeremy opened his eyes. He saw a young man who, though much older than he remembered, was definitely his brother. Jeremy gathered all the energy he had left and was careful to speak clearly.

"Melech," he said, and both men heard him. That seemed to erase his father's doubts, and there was no more argument. He felt his face covered in tears and kisses, and then he felt himself being picked up and carried in someone's arms.

Melech carried him across the river and up the well-remembered hill. He tried to speak and deliver his message about the approaching armies of the Vizier, but Melech only said "Hush," and wouldn't listen. That at least was no surprise, he thought to himself wryly.

Jeremy didn't remember being carried the rest of the way to the house. By then he was in a sleep of such exhaustion that it would have taken much more than that to waken him. He was bathed and dressed in dry clothes, and left to sleep.

He slept all the rest of that day and night, and woke with a start early the next morning. He was sore all over, and thirstier than he could ever remember being in his entire life, but other than that he felt ready to get up. He started to do so, and Melech came in to find him sitting on the edge of the bed. Melech smiled wider than you would think a face could smile, and threw his arms around Jeremy.

Jeremy was more than a little disconcerted by all this. It wasn't the kind of reaction he would have expected from Melech, considering the way he used to act.

"Jeremy, we thought you were dead! Where have you been all this time?" he asked.

Jeremy hesitated to go into all that with Melech right now. Too much of it would sound like boasting, and he hadn't time for talking much right now. He guessed he was barely three days ahead of the Vizier's army, and he'd just wasted one of those days by sleeping. He dared not rest any longer. Therefore he kept his tale to the bare minimum.

"There was a caravan of Sohrab traders camped by the river that day. They caught me and sold me for a slave in Cerise. I was set free soon after, but I lived in that city for many years. I've passed through many dangers and seen so many wonderful and terrible things, Melech, but all that isn't important right now. I passed through the Gap of the Murray in that barrel, because I had such desperate need to hurry. That was how you came to find me on the shoals yesterday. A vast army is crossing the mountains even as we speak, and I must warn King Jonah immediately," Jeremy told him.

"It would take weeks to get to Rustrum, and you can't leave right away!" Melech objected. Jeremy was sad that he couldn't spend more time, but he dared not.

"Melech, I am a prophet of the Most High, and I can't forsake the duty I'm called to do. Please, help me and don't hinder me," he pleaded. Melech bit his lip, and looked searchingly into Jeremy's eyes. What he saw there must have convinced him.

"All right, Jeremy. I'll help," he said softly.

"Thank you," Jeremy told him.

"But you have to make a promise to me, little brother. When you're finished with the work of the Most High, come back here, at least for a little while. The years go by faster than you would think, and we all have missed you so much. You have no idea," Melech sighed. Jeremy pondered this.

"I promise, Melech," he said, "I'll come back for a while, as soon as I can, but for now I have to leave right away."

Melech nodded.

"I understand. Come, then," he said. Jeremy got up from the bed, feeling pain in every muscle, and followed his brother outside. Melech took him to the cattle shed behind the house and introduced him to a donkey who had not been there when Jeremy last visited the place.

"Her name is Binka, and you'll need to ride if you want to make any time. She's not very fast, but better than your own two feet. You can get a real horse once you get down on the Plain. Leave Binka at the inn in Laath, and I'll fetch her when I can," Melech said.

"Melech, tell Papa and Mama goodbye for me, and tell them why I had to hurry," Jeremy said.

"Of course," Melech promised.

Jeremy could spend no more time talking. He mounted Binka and rode quickly out the back gate toward the river. She seemed a placid beast, and that was a good thing indeed. He was still sore and bruised all over from his ride in the barrel. He couldn't take much jostling.

When he came to the river, he noticed that a road now snaked along the bank in both directions. A rough one, to be sure, but a road nonetheless. Jonah had apparently been busy the past few years.

Jeremy rode quickly downstream, getting as much speed out of Binka as he dared. He rode hard and fast all day long and far into the night, only stopping when exhaustion forced him to. He arose before sunrise the next morning and went on, reaching the foot of the Eyre Hills about midmorning. Here the road crossed the Murray at a shallow ford, and beside the river stood what had to be the village of Laath. It hadn't been there when Jeremy last saw the place. Now there was a thriving little town beside the full river, set amid pastures and fields.

He came to the inn (there was only one), and arranged to board the donkey there for a month. It was too much to hope for to find a horse for sale in such a small village, and indeed he didn't find one. But the innkeeper had a riding horse which he was willing to rent. Jeremy had to pay dearly for the use of the beast, and it was agreed that he should ride it no farther than Thaloth.

Jeremy didn't quibble about the matter. He paid the money and took the horse. He had already decided to ride at once to Cerise instead of Rustrum, for Cerise was the city most immediately in danger, and messengers could be sent from there to Rustrum.

Jeremy reached Thaloth in four days, so hard did he push the poor horse. The High Plain was filled with people again, though not nearly so many yet as it had once had. There were still many empty villages. But in all those that were occupied, Jeremy cried out a warning about the army of Lakkaia, which he knew was hard on his heels.

He deposited the innkeeper's horse in Thaloth, and there he was able to buy a good steed of his own. Jeremy wasted an hour at the palace of the Governor, demanding urgently to see the man. He had no luck until he told his right name and threatened to have the Governor and his entire staff thrown into prison before the day was out if he didn't speak to the man *instantly*. Even that didn't produce immediate action, and Jeremy took matters into his own hands by walking briskly into the audience chamber and interrupting some dignitary or other who was speaking to the Governor about taxes.

Jeremy swept the tax man aside and ordered the Governor to prepare for an imminent attack. He gave such details as he knew, and then departed as quickly as he'd come. The Governor was not a sheep-witted fool; Jeremy knew he would at least begin to make preparations for battle, even if he did feel compelled to send scouts to verify what Jeremy had said. Let him do so, and he'd discover the truth of the matter soon enough.

Jeremy rode into Cerise late the next evening. Here, too, he found changes from the last time he'd seen the place. The city seemed less crowded, and cleaner than he remembered. There were more fountains, and blue banners draped from the windows of the Houses along the main street from the east gate to the market square. Jeremy had not forgotten his way around the city, and he went immediately to the House which had once belonged to Amagon. It was now the Earl's House (for that was the title Eli had been given).

Eli was not at home, and Jeremy chafed at the delay. There wasn't time! The chief steward of the household recognized Jeremy immediately, for he had been there since Amagon's days. Eli had kept many of the same servants and councilors; there were only a few new faces. The steward told him that the Earl had gone to Rustrum to consult with the King. In his absence, he had appointed a regent to act on his behalf. This was the King's older brother Joel. Jeremy knew him very well from his visits to Jonah's house long ago. He was a competent man and a trusted advisor, but not very imaginative.

Jeremy rode immediately to the old House of the Satrap, which was where Joel lived. The Regent had already gone to bed by the time Jeremy arrived, but Jeremy didn't hesitate an instant to wake him. The staff of the House all recognized Jeremy and didn't dare interfere.

Joel was snoring when Jeremy walked into the bedchamber and shook him roughly.

"Joel, wake up!" he said urgently.

"What is it?" Joel asked crossly, rolling over to peer at him with sleepy eyes. Then he seemed to recognize who he was looking at, and a grin lit up his face.

"Jeremy! Where have you been all this time? The Earl and my brother the King will be overjoyed to see you!" he began, all trace of sleepiness evaporating. Then he noticed Jeremy's serious expression.

"Is something wrong?" he asked.

"Joel, you need to prepare the city for a siege immediately. A vast army is heading this way even as we speak, less than a week behind me, led by a sorcerer of terrible power. He means to destroy and plunder the entire kingdom if he can, beginning with Cerise. There's not a moment to lose!" Jeremy hissed.

Joel fumbled for his shoes and called for messengers to be sent to wake the rest of the city leaders at once, and for runners to be sent to the battalion at the mines to summon them home to defend the city. Other riders were sent in haste to Rustrum to warn the King and the Earl.

Jeremy and Joel spent a sleepless night in frenzied preparations. Jeremy gathered that the city would be easier to defend than he'd feared. Many people had left the city and the valley lands over the past few years and gone to resettle the High Plain. This meant that not as much food and water would be needed to sustain the city during a siege, for there would be fewer mouths to feed.

The next few days were spent fortifying the walls and gates of the city, and gathering as many of the people of the valley inside the walls as possible, for protection. The battalion which guarded the dye mines arrived at the city on the fourth day after Jeremy, bringing with them the miners and other folk who lived in that place. The mines would be left unguarded for now, but that mattered very little. There was nothing there which could be stolen or destroyed.

Reports began to come in that the High Plain was overrun with enemies, and the Governor and all his people slain, and Thaloth burned to the ground. The army of Lakkaia went to and fro pillaging and destroying everything within reach, and the folk who lived in those regions were fleeing into the hills and down from the Plain by whatever ways they could find.

Eli reached Cerise six days after Jeremy, and they were glad in the midst of their troubles.

"You return at last, old friend," Eli told him warmly.

"I only wish it could have been under better circumstances, and with better news to bear," Jeremy said wryly. Eli laughed.

"Oh, but imagine what would have happened if you *hadn't* come, though," Eli said, "I'd much rather hear bad news than return home to a pile of smoking ashes."

"That's as like as not to be the case even now, if help doesn't come that I can't foresee," Jeremy pointed out grimly. Eli didn't deny it.

"Maybe, but then again maybe not. The city is strong, and the invaders may have a harder time than they imagine. And if we fall, then we must commit ourselves to the Most High. In either case, we have nothing to fear," Eli said.

He paused for a minute, as if thinking about the coming battle. Then he smiled again.

"Come now, the city is as ready as it can be, and all we can do now is wait. Tell me where you've been all this time, and what you've been doing, and where Daniel may be. There's plenty of time to think of blood and battle whenever it arrives, and for now I'd rather think on good things as long as I'm allowed," he said.

Jeremy couldn't disagree, and he told the story of his journeys at full length. Eli never seemed to grow weary of even the smallest details. Jeremy was so busy remembering the past that he had no time to think about the present danger. Maybe that was the intention, for Eli had become an excellent leader of men, who knew very well how to encourage those around him.

They talked far into the night, and then Jeremy found that he could sleep, although he would have thought that was impossible only a few hours earlier.

## Chapter Twenty
### Dreams and Doubts

During the night, the army of Lakkaia flowed down from the High Plain in an endless stream, filling the valley with a black sea of enemies. The defenders on the walls of Cerise saw the enemy torches in the night stretching from horizon to horizon, and they shivered.

Then the sun rose, and all hope died. The defenders were outnumbered a hundred to one or more.

A siege is a dull thing, for the most part. Not much happens for long periods of time, except for occasional skirmishes. This one was a little different because everyone knew it couldn't last very long. The Lakkaian army was too large to support itself by plunder, so they meant to take the city as soon as possible. They were a long way from home, and one of the things Joel had been most careful to do was to order that no food of any type be left outside the city walls, even if that meant it had to be destroyed.

The Vizier seemed to recognize the position he was in, and took action accordingly. He sent waves of attackers with ladders to climb the walls, while bowmen shot clouds of arrows at the defenders. Many of the ladders were thrown off the wall and fell down in splinters among the attackers, but as soon as one ladder was thrown back, three more took its place.

The fighting was hottest near the gates, since the Vizier's best hope was to capture one of them and throw it open to his army. The soldiers of Cerise were soon tired to the point of exhaustion, for they dared not rest an instant. The Vizier kept up the assault constantly.

"It's only a matter of time until the city is destroyed, Jeremy," Eli said, in a rare moment of quiet at the Earl's House. They had returned there from the city walls only a short time before. Jeremy nodded.

"That much is clear, Eli, but I see nothing to do about it except die as bravely as we can when the time comes," he said.

"It's not like you to be so grim," Eli said after a pause.

"Maybe not, but can you think of anything yourself?" Jeremy asked. Eli hesitated.

"Perhaps a flood. . ." he suggested.

"It would only destroy the city right along with the attackers, I'm afraid. The valley is too narrow in this place," Jeremy said bleakly. There was another long pause.

"If that's true, then I think I would rather have it so than to watch the city burn at the hands of the Lakkaians," Eli said quietly. Jeremy pondered this.

"I'm not sure you quite understand. A flood big enough to destroy the army would not only wash away Cerise. It would also lay waste to the entire valley. Maybe even destroy Rustrum when the water reached that point. I just don't know," he said.

"And yet the other choice seems to be certain destruction anyway," Eli pointed out. Jeremy thought about this for a while, but found no solution. He looked up at Eli.

"I don't know what to say, Eli. I can't believe that the Most High would have brought us all through so much, or let us accomplish so much, if He only meant to let it all be destroyed and forgotten. I don't know what He will do, but I refuse to accept the idea that all is lost," Jeremy said. Eli smiled wryly.

"I know you're right. I just wish I knew what to do," he said.

"So do we all," Jeremy sighed.

That ended any talk about miracles, at least for the time being. Jeremy left the room and walked wearily to his bed chamber, in the hope of getting at least a few hours of sleep. He knew it wasn't likely to turn out that way, that someone would probably wake him up within thirty minutes to handle some emergency or other, but he was so bone-tired by then that he didn't much care.

While he trudged down the hall, he thought about the strange sorcerer who called himself the Vizier of Lakkaia. What did he want? What exactly did he hope to gain by destroying Rustrum? Jeremy knew well enough that it was much too far away from Lakkaia for the Vizier to have any hope of conquering the land and actually keeping it. It would cost more than it was worth. And yet, what other motive could there be? It couldn't be from self-defense, for the Vizier knew perfectly well that Rustrum was no threat to him. So what was it? Jeremy puzzled and puzzled, trying to figure out what was behind it all. If he could grasp the Vizier's purposes, he might be able to think of a way to thwart them.

Presently he came to his bed and lay down without even taking his clothes off, and he was asleep the moment his head touched the pillow.

Sometime during that long night of fear, Jeremy had a dream. He seemed to be standing on the edge of the High Plain, looking down on the valley from somewhere near Cerise. There was a bright moon in the sky, which glittered on the water of the river. The sands of the desert beyond were spectral and still, without even a breath of wind to stir them. The army of Lakkaia surrounded Cerise almost as far as he could see in either direction. It seemed to him (though he didn't know why) that Maia was standing beside him, and she soon leaned close to whisper in his ear, "Remember your enemy." He thought to ask her what she meant, but before he could do it he snapped awake.

He lay alone on the floor beside his bed, as wide awake as he could ever remember being. The dream was still fresh in his mind, and he wondered if it meant anything.

Jeremy pulled himself up off the floor, cold and stiff from lying on the hard wood for so long. He wasn't sure exactly how many hours had passed since he fell asleep, but the night felt almost spent. The air coming in through the open window had the unmistakable smell of early morning, even though there wasn't yet the faintest trace of light in the sky. It was much warmer in Cerise than it had been on the north side of the mountains, and the taste of early spring was already in the air.

He went quietly to the basin beneath the mirror and splashed his face with water, furrowing his brow as he thought about the dream. What did it mean to remember his enemy? Jeremy himself had no enemies, as far as he knew. At least no personal ones. He might once have thought of Melech as an enemy, but not really anymore. King Joseph was long gone, and nobody in Rustrum was sorry about that. So who was left?

He continued to think about the matter as he left the room and headed purposefully down the hall to talk to Joel and Eli and hear whatever news there might be. He must have had a faraway look in his eyes, for no one spoke to him before he reached the council chamber. By that time he had decided there could be only one person the dream was referring to. The Vizier of Lakkaia, the leader of the army that meant to destroy Rustrum, and the man who had corrupted almost an entire nation. The Lakkaians themselves would never have attacked anyone, if not for the Vizier. Jeremy was certain of his conclusion, but that still left him wondering what he was supposed to do about it. How did it help to know exactly who the enemy was, if there wasn't any way to defeat him?

While he considered these things, a new thought came into his mind; one he didn't like much. The city was lost unless something drastic happened, and there was no obvious sign of that. All the armies of Rustrum put together could never withstand the invaders. But where the many fail, it sometimes happens that a single person may succeed. Especially when, as now, there was no hope left anyway.

The council chamber was deserted when he reached it, and Jeremy quietly returned to his rooms and put on a plain brown tunic and a hood to cover his head and face. He was glad it was still cool outside, since no one would think it was strange to be wearing such heavy clothing. He took no weapon with him. . . nothing but a verse from the Book of the Prophets, clasped tight in his left hand. Then he made his way as silently as he could to the Builder's Hall. It wasn't possible to escape the city without being noticed and almost certainly killed, but Jeremy had been in that situation before.

He saw no one as he approached the tunnel mouth that led down to the aqueduct, and he breathed a sigh of relief when he entered the darkness of the tunnel. Then he heard the most unwelcome sound he could possibly have encountered at that moment- the sharp intake of someone's breath.

"Who goes there?" he demanded harshly, afraid his whole plan was falling apart before it even got started.

"Only old Marah, Lord, and I'm no harm to ye," he heard a papery old voice say. That wasn't good.

"Lady, if you value the life of your city and mine and yours as well, forget you ever saw me here tonight," he told her. His eyes had adjusted to the darkness now, and he could see her lying on a pile of something at the side of the tunnel in her filthy skirts, with long stringy gray hair that made her look very old. But her eyes were bright when she looked up at him, betraying no trace of confusion.

"So you say. Let's see the color of your coin, and then we'll talk," the old woman said, with a crafty smile. Jeremy could hardly believe it for a minute. Did she really think she could rob him? He hardly had time for the thought to pass through his head before the old lady gave a loud whistle, and with a rustling and whispering sound several unfriendly-looking beggars from the slums of Cerise surrounded him. Some of them showed the glint of steel in the moonlight. The old lady cackled at his alarm.

"Thought you could ignore an old woman, eh? Thought you could just kick us aside and go your way, did you? Ye big dandy," she said scornfully.

"Take him, boys!" she ordered.

Jeremy had found himself in more than one tight spot in his life, but never had he felt so afraid as he did that night, alone and weaponless, among people who obviously cared no more about killing him than they would about swatting a fly. He prepared himself to go down fighting, if that's the way it had to be. He had learned a little about bare-handed combat during his time as a page, but he knew perfectly well he was no match for a half dozen men with daggers and knives. He could hope for nothing better than to hurt a few of them fairly badly before he lost the battle. The rabble evidently expected as much, and they were hanging back for the moment, each one of them seeming reluctant to be the first one to wade in and get hurt.

One of them finally did, and with a yell came at Jeremy with his knife raised. Jeremy jumped aside and kicked him in the ribs, which sent the man writhing in pain onto the brick floor with the breath knocked out of him. The others murmured angrily, but they were wary.

Jeremy noticed that all but one of them were blocking the mouth of the tunnel. They probably expected him to try to escape that way, and the one man between him and the deeper parts of the tunnel didn't seem to be either the largest or the strongest. Jeremy thought he saw an opportunity. He pretended to lunge for the tunnel mouth, but it was only a feint. Before the men realized what he was doing, Jeremy had knocked the one man down and was running like mad into the depths of the tunnel. He hadn't escaped without injury, for the man had managed to give him a sharp cut across the front of his calf. He could feel a trickle of warm blood running down into his shoe and making his foot sticky. Nor had the robbers given up. They were after him, almost at his heels, yelling and cursing and promising horrible vengeance as soon as they caught him.

It was too much to hope that he might get away. Before long, he felt a strong hand grab his hood from behind, almost tearing it off. He had no choice but to turn and fight the man, knife or no knife. If the two of them had been alone, Jeremy might have had a chance, but that situation didn't last very long. Within a few seconds the other robbers came running up, and it wasn't long before one of them kicked Jeremy's feet out from under him. He fell hard on the pavement stones, knocking the breath out of him. He tried to get back up, but before he could do anything he felt the cold tickle of steel at his throat, and he froze.

"That's right, dandy. . . keep still," he heard one of the men panting.

They didn't hurt him immediately, which was better than Jeremy had expected. One of them dragged out a bundle of cords and tied up his hands and feet. It was carelessly done, and Jeremy thought he could probably get out of them sooner or later, but it would take a while. They seemed to be waiting for something, but Jeremy couldn't guess what. One of them lit a lamp of some kind, the better to see what Jeremy had. They rummaged through his few belongings (he expected that), and seemed angry when they found no money or valuables. He could hear them muttering and cursing under their breath while they pawed his things, every once in a while there came the sound of something hitting the floor when it was either dropped or tossed aside. None of them said a word to him.

Eventually they got tired of looking and most of them headed back up the tunnel. Not without a few black looks at Jeremy, to be sure, but he was relieved to see the last of them. Or almost the last. The man who had grabbed Jeremy's hood hung back, and after the others were quite out of sight, he came up to Jeremy and looked at him with a hard glare. But there was also a sort of hungry look there, if Jeremy guessed right.

"What's your name, dandy?" the young man finally asked, tensely. Jeremy knew lots of reasons not to give out his name, but in this case he decided he had nothing to lose.

"I am Jeremy, the Prophet," he finally said, looking up at his captor. He thought he saw a glint of recognition in the man's eyes.

"Are you really, then? Prove it," he scoffed. Jeremy looked at him steadily.

"I have no way to do that; not here, and you should know that the Most High is not like a circus bear, that He should do tricks to satisfy your curiosity," he said. The man looked angry for a minute, then seemed to think better of it. Instead, he yanked back Jeremy's hood, catching some of the hair in his fist also. Jeremy bit his tongue at the pain, but wouldn't give the man the satisfaction of seeing him yelp.

However, the man seemed to have had a sudden change of heart.

"Were you once the master of pages in Lord Amagon's house?" the man demanded. This was not a question Jeremy had expected, but he answered frankly,

"Yes, but that was a long time ago," he replied. The robber took this in, lost in thought for a moment.

"I believe you," he finally said, slowly, "There could be no other who looked the same." He let go of Jeremy's hair and became much more respectful.

"My family is in your debt, Lord. You may remember my brother Mimelech; you gave him a place to serve in the House for several years," the man went on.

Jeremy didn't remember the name, but that wasn't surprising. There had been so many pages in the House over the years. However, he wisely said nothing about this, waiting to see what came of it.

"And is he well now?" Jeremy ventured to ask. A look of sorrow passed across the man's face.

"I fear not, Lord. He was able to join the Guard after he left your House, and we have heard nothing of him these past several days, since the city was surrounded," he said. Jeremy wondered how it was possible for a thief and a robber to have a brother who was in the City Guard, but then he dismissed the question. It didn't matter, and it wasn't his business anyway.

"The city will fall any day. I have a plan to save it, but I can't do that if I'm tied up here. Will you let me go?" Jeremy asked. The man hesitated, obviously not liking that idea much.

"The others would wonder how it happened, and I fear they would kill me if they found out," the man said.

"Then you must come with me," Jeremy said firmly. The man hesitated again.

"No, Lord, I couldn't do that. But I will let you go, all the same. Marah will understand, when I tell her who you are. At least I think she will," the man said. He sounded a bit doubtful, but nevertheless he took out a knife and cut the cords which bound Jeremy's hands and feet. Jeremy stood up, and looked the man squarely in the eye.

"You're a brave man, and it may be that you've saved your own life as well as the city tonight. I thank you," he said.

"Thank the Most High," the man said, with a crooked smile, and before Jeremy could say anything else, he turned and walked swiftly away, back up the tunnel.

Jeremy didn't linger. He turned on his heel and hurried down the tunnel as quickly as he could safely go. He soon heard the sound of the water flowing in the aqueduct. It filled him with more than a little fear. The aqueduct was not an ankle-deep trickle anymore, but a full stream. He discovered this fact when he came to the end of the tunnel. The water filled the aqueduct to within a foot of the roof. There didn't seem to be much current, but that could be deceptive.

Jeremy hesitated for a minute before wading into the stream, but he set his jaw and determined to do it in spite of the danger. He felt a freezing shock of cold when he entered the water, and that was another worry. Going swimming this early in the year was hardly a safe thing to do for very long.

He found that the water came up to his chin when he reached the main bore of the pipe, with only a mild current to push him along. As he remembered, the water level in the pipe varied from place to place. There were times when it sank to chest height, and other times when it rose to within an inch or two of the roof. Those places were scary. Jeremy had to hold his breath as he half-walked and half-swam, then tilt his head back and stick his nose up against the ceiling tiles just to take a breath. He dragged his fingers above his head the whole time just to make sure there was still any air at all.

He was soon so cold that his body was shivering violently, and that didn't make things any easier. He also found that the current was picking up speed as he went along, so that it became harder and harder to keep his footing.

All during that journey in the darkness and the freezing cold, he tried not to let himself think about what would happen if the water ever reached the ceiling completely. He didn't know if he had the strength to struggle upstream against the current until he reached the tunnel mouth again. And even if he did, then the city was lost.

He almost stopped feeling the cold after a while, and even though he knew that was a bad sign, he welcomed it anyway. He walked along in a daze for quite some time, forgetting to count his steps. There came a point when the current grew strong enough to sweep him off his weary legs, and before much longer, the water filled the entire bore of the pipe.

Jeremy barely had time to notice these things before he was sucked under for the last time.

### Chapter Twenty-One
### *Battle*

The current rushed him headlong through the pipe. He held his breath as best he could as the water tumbled him over and over like a ball of string.

It seemed like forever, but in fact it was only a little more than a minute that Jeremy was caught up in the pipe. Then, without warning, he shot out the mouth of the pipe into a place he vaguely realized must be the river. He was still several feet under water, but he could see the early morning sunlight shimmering on the surface of the water not far above him. The cold seemed to have seeped into his very bones, and he could hardly make his muscles work to swim. His lungs were screaming for air, and he knew in a fuzzy kind of way that he didn't have much longer to live if he didn't get out of the water. He decided it would be a foolish thing to survive the trip down the aqueduct just to drown in the river within sight of shore. He summoned all the strength he had left in his body, and struggled toward the light he saw. At last his head popped up to the surface, and he took deep gasping breaths to fight off the blackness that threatened to overpower him. He knew if he fainted, he was lost.

Soon his head cleared a bit, and he saw that he wasn't in fact very far from the bank. The river had carried him a fair distance downstream, but not so much as he might have thought. He could still see the city about a mile upstream.

He struggled to the shore and crawled out onto a rock, with water pouring off him. There was patchy frost on the grass, and Jeremy could never remember being so cold in his entire life. He scooted up against a dirt embankment and wrung out his clothes as best he could. He knew better than to sit still, even as tired as he was. That was how people froze to death. He started walking downstream, as briskly as he could manage. He was too cold and sick to go very fast. He didn't dare build a fire, even if he'd had the materials to do it with, for fear of attracting attention. There didn't seem to be any Lakkaian soldiers in the vicinity, but he could see their watchfires clearly, not much farther upstream. They would certainly be able to see his, if he lit one. Therefore he chose caution, and wrapped his arms as tightly around his body as he could. There was at least no wind.

The sun gave little warmth so early in the morning. He was shivering violently, but he knew that was a good thing. It meant his body was regaining some heat.

Before much longer, he came to a little patch of oak woods. They were black oaks, of the kind that didn't drop their leaves till the new buds opened in spring. Jeremy was glad for the cover. He ducked inside the edge of the woods, and it wasn't long before he came across a woodcutter's cottage. It was deserted, but that didn't surprise him. All the folk who lived in the countryside had run as fast and as far as they could. He had to pick up a rock and break open the lock on the front door, an act of vandalism for which he silently asked the owner's forgiveness. But he was afraid if he didn't find a place to hide and get warm, he might not be strong enough to do what he needed to do.

He slipped into the cottage and quietly shut the door behind him. A quick search turned up dry clothes that were only a little too big for him, and he changed into these gratefully. There was also a blanket on the bed, and he wrapped himself in this as well. Further investigation turned up a block of hard cheese in one of the cupboards, and a slightly moldy loaf of rye bread. He couldn't find a knife to cut either of them, but he was not above taking bites off the main portion at this point. He took the food to bed with him, not caring at all whether he got crumbs on the sheets. Then he wrapped himself in every blanket and piece of clothing he could find, and slept.

He woke about mid afternoon, feeling sick. He sat up, bleary eyed and still weary, blinking to try to see clearly. When he finally did, he almost wished he were still asleep. He ate some more cheese and bread and drank a little water, then got up. He ached in every muscle, and he found soon enough that the bed was infested with fleas. Jeremy was tempted to curse the woodcutter, but on the other hand he was eating the man's food and sleeping in his house without being invited, so maybe it wasn't fair to be too harsh.

He got up from the bed, scratching himself in a dozen places, and sat at the table instead. There were no windows in the cottage, but he opened the door a bit and let in a shaft of golden sun. He guessed it was about three o'clock by the slant of the light. Not much time left.

Jeremy rid himself of as many fleas as he could easily find, wrapped himself in one of the blankets as a kind of shawl, and left the cottage. He took the remainder of the bread and cheese with him, just in case. There was no telling when he might be able to find food again. His shoes were still soaking wet, but that couldn't be helped.

When he was as ready as he could be, he stepped outside the door and latched it shut again as well as he could. He made a mental note to repay the woodcutter for the damage as soon as possible.

The oak leaves were rustling and whispering in a light breeze when he left the cottage, but it was a fairly warm and sunny afternoon. It was so peaceful and quiet, it was hard to believe a desperate war was going on less than a mile away. It was even harder for Jeremy to believe that he was actually walking straight into that war zone, without even a weapon. He wondered if his plan was quite as stupid as it seemed, but then he decided that was in the hands of the Most High.

It took him about an hour to reach the outskirts of the Lakkaian camp, and at that point he had to make a decision. Should he show himself to the soldiers and ask to be taken to the Vizier? That was certainly the most direct and straightforward thing, but was there any hope the soldiers would really do it? They might try to throw him in prison or even kill him. Jeremy had no fear of these things, (or not much, anyway), but he did fear delay. The city might be overrun at any time, and then all would be lost.

The other idea was to try to sneak through the camp until he reached the Vizier's tent. That wasn't ideal either, since he was almost certain to be caught sometime before he got there, and then the soldiers would be even less likely to do what he asked. Also, that would take more time.

Jeremy gritted his teeth. Why did things have to be so difficult?

He decided soon enough there was no time for delay. The soldiers would just have to do whatever they chose to do. Accordingly, he walked boldly toward the outskirts of the camp, with his head held high and his jaw set firmly. He expected to be challenged almost immediately, and he was surprised when that didn't happen. Nobody seemed to be guarding the camp, and the soldiers he saw were loafing around their tents playing dice and drinking ale. None of them paid him any attention. He wondered if they were already so sure of victory that they didn't feel the need to even post guards, or if they were so uninterested in the war that they felt comfortable ignoring it.

For a while, he assumed that these troops on the outskirts of the camp were the strays and wastrels of the army, the unimportant and unwilling ones who cared little about the war. He knew perfectly well that the soldiers near the city were of a different sort altogether. Those ones meant business.

But as he wandered deeper into the camp, he realized it wasn't just a few lazy stragglers who weren't paying attention. The lack of discipline and order was everywhere. Jeremy was shocked that the Vizier would think of invading another country with such a weak and disorganized rabble as this. They looked fearsome from a distance, but the more he saw of the Lakkaian army, the more inclined he was to laugh at them. Then he remembered what they had already done to the High Plain, and it wasn't funny anymore.

He thought of Maia, and decided what he ought to do.

Some of the platoons were larger than others, and Jeremy chose a largish one that seemed to have more drinking going on than usual. He elbowed his way into the crowd as if he belonged there, and as he expected no one challenged him. The men were circled around two soldiers, who seemed to be in a fighting match. No one seemed to mind, for he could overhear bets and cheers of encouragement from the spectators. He joined in, lest he seem out of place, but all the time he watched carefully. There seemed to be no rules to the fight- both men had no scruples about taking any advantage they saw, pulling hair, jabbing at eyes, kicking and scratching like cats. Both of them were covered in blood and sweat, so the fight must have been going on for some time.

It didn't take much longer before one of the men got careless, and the other delivered a bone-cracking punch to his chest. Even over the noise of the crowd, Jeremy could hear the sound of ribs breaking. No game, then. The man howled in pain and fell to the ground. A couple of others quickly dragged him aside into a tent, while the rest cheered the victor. He was a huge man, and seemed little the worse for wear after knocking down his opponent. Indeed, he soon began shaking his fist at the crowd and challenging anyone who dared to fight him. No one seemed eager to try it, though they were content to cheer him on. Jeremy took a deep breath and stepped forward.

"I'll fight you," he said. The man was almost twice his size, and when he heard Jeremy's challenge he laughed. Some of the crowd did, too, but not all. As usual, there were always some who cheered for the underdog.

The man laughed again. "Go home, runt, and don't be a fool," he said. Jeremy stood up a little straighter.

"Afraid, then?" he taunted, with what he hoped was a sneer on his face. The crowd hushed, breathless with anticipation. The giant looked astonished for a minute, then his face turned red with fury.

"Come on then, runt. Taste my fists," he said, and charged Jeremy immediately.

This was a mistake, for Jeremy had plenty of time to jump aside. People usually thought size and strength were all it took to win a fight, but these were not enough without good leverage. Jeremy remembered his combat lessons very well.

The crowd booed when they saw him jump out of the way, calling him a coward and worse things, but he paid no attention to that. Before the big man could turn around, Jeremy leaped up on his back and got a tight hold around his neck. In that position, the man couldn't use his size or strength at all. He tried, though. Jeremy found blows raining down on him from both sides, but they lacked force. The man grabbed his hair and pulled hard. Jeremy gritted his teeth at the pain, but didn't let go his grip around the man's throat. Before long the handful of hair came tearing out, and the man threw it on the ground. He swung around, trying to dislodge Jeremy from his position. But although his legs swung around crazily and he was almost torn loose, he kept his grip, slowly tightening it as quickly as he could. The man started gasping for breath, but he was far from beaten yet. A lucky blow hit Jeremy squarely on the left ear, and a ring or something on the man's hand gashed his skin. Soon his hair and hood were matted with blood from the cut. Sweat ran down into his eyes and stung, and he was afraid if the man didn't give up soon he might lose his grip. Swimming in the icy river all night had sapped his strength considerably.

The man tried to grab another fistful of hair, but succeeded only in ripping Jeremy's hood completely off. Jeremy tightened his hold around the man's throat to the point that it felt like his arms would break, but he was beginning to have an effect. The man's punches were getting weaker, and just when he thought he couldn't hold on a minute longer, the man under him collapsed heavily to the ground, twitching and gasping for air. Jeremy let go of him and stood up with his foot on the man's neck, then raised his fist in the air and gave a yell of victory. The crowd cheered just as loud as they had booed earlier, and several rushed in and picked him up on their shoulders to carry him around the camp. He was apparently a celebrity.

Someone opened a fresh cask of beer, and his new fans poured the first glass over his head. He didn't let it show how much it hurt when the alcohol flooded over his ripped ear. He knew what came next. He was handed another glass, and the crowd quieted down to hear what he would say. Nearly a hundred expectant faces looked up at him, holding their glasses till he drank first. This was the moment he'd been waiting for, and if he blew it he probably wouldn't live to get a second chance.

"Men of Lakkaia, I salute you! It's an honor to serve with you all!" he began. He was interrupted by enthusiastic cheers and banging of weapons on shields. There were a few who drained their glasses, since he'd obviously said everything that needed saying, but most were paying enough attention to see that he wasn't done yet. These quieted the other rowdies down, and soon he had their attention again. He dared not speak too long lest he lose their interest, so he did the one thing that was guaranteed to shock them most.

"Glory and honor to the Most High forever!" he shouted. Instantly there was dead silence, and he thought he saw a few men's mouths drop open. Such words carried the penalty of death, and all knew it.

Before the men could recover from their astonishment, Jeremy quickly went on.

"Men of Lakkaia, I know well that the Grand Vizier, that evil sorcerer, has forbidden those words, and I know the lies he has told you. I know how he forced you all to come here to a foreign land whose people have never done you any harm, and that if you could, you would much rather be in your homes today. Know then, I am Jeremy, a Prophet of the Most High, and I have come to destroy him and all who follow him, and set your land free. All who follow me will not lack for a reward!"

There was some feeble cheering at this, but most of the men just looked scared, and a few seemed furious. Several gripped their swords and rushed toward him with a look in their eyes that meant certain death if they reached him. Jeremy looked up to the sky.

"Father, show them," he prayed at the top of his lungs.

The black clouds gathered instantly in the sunny sky, and rain began to fall. A few of his attackers threw down their weapons and wailed in terror, but three of the most hardened ones looked more determined than ever. Jeremy stood his ground, unflinching. Just before the men reached him, when their swords were already raised to slash him, the lightning came. A fiery bolt consumed the attackers on the spot, leaving nothing but smoking ashes and melted steel where they had stood just a moment before. All the men had seen it, and none of them looked eager to attack him again. Most of them looked either terrified or awe-struck.

"The same thing will happen to any who oppose the Most High. Join me and destroy the Vizier, or be destroyed along with him! Choose!" Jeremy commanded. His voice swayed the men nearby, and first one and then nearly all of them began to cheer and then chant "Down with the Vizier! Glory to the Most High!"

### *Chapter Twenty-Two*
### *Endings, and Beginnings*

Word spread like wildfire in the Lakkaian camp. Many of the soldiers had been secret followers of the Most High, and when they heard that a prophet had come to destroy the Vizier, all these deserted their posts and came over to Jeremy's camp.

There was soon a fierce battle raging between the two parts of the Lakkaian army. Cerise was forgotten for a time, and Eli and the other defenders looked out in dumbfounded amazement as their attackers suddenly began fighting each other like a hive of ants that had been stirred with a stick.

Jeremy had quickly shed his flea-infested tunic in favor of Lakkaian battle armor and a sword. Lightning struck again and again on the battlefield, and the terror this inspired among the Vizier's soldiers was very great, so that more and more of them deserted to fight on Jeremy's side.

But Jeremy had not forgotten the Vizier himself, and he knew full well that the old sorcerer had something up his sleeve, for he hadn't appeared at all in the battle yet. When he did, it was worse than Jeremy had feared.

He stood atop a war elephant and hurled flame at Jeremy's soldiers, destroying whole platoons with each burst. He was not harmed by the lightning, and his fire was crushing Jeremy's army.

Jeremy reached up his arms to the sky, and the rain began to fall in torrents. That put an end to the Vizier's fireballs, but not to the battle. A lightning bolt struck the war elephant, and it screamed as it fell to the ground, crushing several men underneath its bulk.

But not the Vizier. He leaped free of the falling beast and landed on the ground nearby, slipping in the mud but keeping his ground.

The battle raged on for hours in this way, with first one side and then the other gaining the advantage. Jeremy fought until his sword was dull as a butterknife and his arms felt like lead. The ground was so muddy that falling was a constant danger.

It came about in the end that Jeremy was fighting the Vizier himself. He had somehow known it would come to that, in the end. In spite of his weariness, he almost welcomed the challenge.

"Well met, young master," the Vizier said with a cold smile. He never took his eyes off Jeremy's face, and this was distracting. Jeremy knew better than to talk and fight at the same time, and he kept his eyes on the Vizier's sword tip, but he couldn't resist making a comment now and then.

"Well met indeed, old monster," he said, with a savage swipe at the Vizier's face. The Vizier laughed and batted him away like a fly that annoyed him. He didn't seem weary at all, and that scared Jeremy a little. He had very little strength left for a prolonged fight.

But prolonged it was, and the exertion began to wear Jeremy down. He gave the Vizier a cut on the right shoulder that kept him from using that arm, but the Vizier, unfazed, simply switched to his left arm. He seemed equally agile with it as he had with the other one. Jeremy himself suffered a deep slash on his left side and several smaller cuts. There was no doubt about who was the better swordsman in this contest, and Jeremy was barely managing to defend himself.

That was bad. It meant sooner or later the Vizier would find a weak spot and get him, if he didn't do something about it.

In the meantime, though, things were happening on the field that neither of them were quite aware of. With the Vizier's attention occupied with Jeremy, he had no time to work his sorcery. More than two-thirds of the troops had deserted him, and although the battle was still fierce in places, the outcome was no longer in doubt. The invasion was over.

Unless, that was, the Vizier somehow managed to kill Jeremy. If he did, the rebels might rejoin him after all, and that would wreck everything.

The battle elsewhere fizzled out into a dozen isolated pockets of fighting, and still Jeremy and the Vizier fought. Jeremy had lost so much blood that he was light-headed, and the fight began to seem more like a dream than reality. He hardly noticed when the far-off sound of the horn on the city gates blared, or when Eli led his exhausted troops out to join the rebels in mopping up the last resistance.

The Vizier soon caught him in a careless moment, and swung his heavy sword and smashed the side of Jeremy's head. Only with the flat, or that would have been the end of him. But the blow dazed him, so that he fell to his knees in the mud, with blood and rain running down his face. The sorcerer was too much for him, after all.

The Vizier looked down at him for a minute in satisfaction, then threw back his head to laugh before finishing him off.

That laugh was his undoing, for in the one moment when his throat was unguarded, a red arrow sped out of nowhere and buried itself through his neck. The Vizier's eyes flew open in shocked surprise, and he staggered backwards. He clutched at the arrow, gave one last look of disbelief at Jeremy, then fell dead in the mud.

Jeremy couldn't believe it himself, and stared stupidly at the body of the Vizier while the rain splashed mud on his armor.

Almost as an afterthought, he waved a hand to stop the rain. It slacked off to a drizzle, and in a few minutes a watery gleam of sun broke through the clouds.

Jeremy struggled to his feet, aching in every muscle. No one seemed to be taking any notice of him or the body of the Vizier. He might have thought that was strange, if he'd stopped to think at all, but in truth he was too weary to care. He stood there, unsmiling, and supposed that in a minute he would head for the city and see if he could find Eli. But not just yet.

While these vague thoughts were passing through his mind, he noticed a young soldier approaching him, with a hood on his head and a bow slung across his back. He supposed this was the man who shot the Vizier and saved his life, and he waited till he came closer to thank him.

When he came within about fifteen feet, the soldier threw back his hood. There, never more beautiful before or after, and certainly never more unexpected, stood Maia. Jeremy was struck speechless. Anything he thought to say seemed utterly inadequate.

"Cat got your tongue?" she asked, and smiled. He smiled back, a bit stupidly, and raised his arms. She ran to him then, and there in the middle of the bloody and rain-soaked field, they held each other for a long time. There were tears, and kisses, and they cared not at all who might see them.

Presently, they linked hands and began the slow walk back to Cerise. There was so much to do, Jeremy hardly wanted to think about it. But in the meantime, neither of them was in any hurry.

"How did you get here?" Jeremy finally asked, shaking his head in amazement. Maia smiled.

"It wasn't hard, you know. I followed along behind the army, and slipped into camp one night when nobody was watching. You might have noticed they didn't keep very good watch. I put on armor, and a hood so no one could tell I wasn't a soldier, and so I came here when everyone else came here. I knew you'd be in the thick of the battle, and I had to make sure you were safe, after all," she said, a little shyly.

"But you didn't even know if I made it through the Gap or not," Jeremy pointed out. She looked at him seriously.

"I knew you made it through," she said.

"But how?" he insisted.

"I just knew it, that's all," she said simply. Jeremy wasn't sure how logical that was, but he smiled anyway.

"Well, I'm glad you came," he said sincerely. She held his hand a little tighter, and together they walked through the gates of Cerise.

In later years, Jeremy looked back often on the strange and crooked path the Most High had laid for him. He and Maia took up residence in Amagon's old House. . . a gift to them by the grateful King and Earl, and there they lived long in blessedness. Jeremy never got a title. . . he was simply the Prophet, and as Jonah said, there was no honor he could give to surpass that one.

The old King of Lakkaia had sworn eternal friendship with the people of Rustrum, when it was known that the Vizier was no more. Many of the soldiers had begged hard at first for Jeremy to come and be their King instead. He would not do this, however, merely remarking that it wasn't his calling. When the old King passed away a few years later, it was Maia's eldest brother who was elected to take his place, no doubt partly because of his connection to Jeremy.

When several years more had passed, Daniel came marching down out of the mountains at the head of a thousand Lachishites, barbarians no longer, but devoted servants of the Most High. The groves of Marithe and Cesme were gone, the blood-worship crushed. Daniel was now King of all the mountains, and a kinder and merrier realm the world had never seen. And so the danger from that quarter was laid to rest.

And so it was that the Three Kingdoms entered a time of peace and happiness such as they had never known. Jeremy was beloved in all three lands, held in reverence by the people and their Kings both. He had only to speak the word, and it was done. And though he seldom ever exercised the power granted to him, he never ceased to marvel at the things the Most High had used him to accomplish. All his daydreams had come true, if not quite in the way he first thought, back in the days when he was a poor cow boy in the Eyre hills.

Maia put it best, when he ventured to speak of these things. It humbled him too much to discuss it with anyone else, but she had a way of seeing things in just the right way. With love in her eyes, she simply laughed and said "Be careful what you wish for!"

He couldn't agree more.

## The End

## Author's Note

The ways in which a story grows from the original seed are sometimes hard to trace, especially after the fact. This one began a long time ago, probably twenty years or more, with a man whose name I'll probably never know. It was a rainy afternoon in Arkadelphia, Arkansas, and I had stopped for a minute under the shelter of a drugstore awning on my way to the library. But while I waited for the rain to slack off a little, I saw the strangest thing. Standing right in the middle of Clinton Street in the soaking rain, was a man in overalls lifting up his face and his hands to the sky and praying aloud. I watched him till he finished his praying and disappeared around the corner, and I've never seen him again since that day. But the image has always remained in my mind, and from that little seed (in the fullness of time) grew this book.

That said, there have been many people since then who gave me germs of ideas and inspiration, and without whom this book wouldn't be what it is. I couldn't begin to name all of them, but here are a few:

Hunter, who gave me a face for Jeremy, and Mickael, who gave me his noble heart. Thanks, guys- I owe you a lot!

Brianna, who will always be my image of Maia.

Katherine, who shared the dream of this book with me for so many years and through so many hard times. I wish we could share this day together, babe, like we always thought we would. *Je me souviens, ma plus chère et ma seule.*

Nathan, Elisabeth, and Mathew, for reminding me what really matters and what doesn't, and for giving me courage when I felt like giving up. I love y'all.

Brandon, for making me laugh when I needed it most. I love you too, BB.

Jeremy, for letting me borrow his name, even though I didn't know it at the time. Peace, little bro.

My mother, for teaching me to write and to love the written word. I couldn't have done it without you, Mama.

My brother, for never letting me take myself or my work too seriously.

And most of all I thank God, the Author of all stories, for this chance to praise His name. Dear Father, let my words speak Truth, and be a glory unto Thee.

William Woodall,
February 12, 2008

## About the Author

William Woodall is a teacher, author, and businessman with deep roots in the evangelical Christian community. He began writing at the age of seven, while watching his mother compose poetry at the kitchen table. That small beginning developed into a lifelong love of books that continues to this day. His self-described literary influences include C.S. Lewis, J.R.R. Tolkien, and George MacDonald. Mr. Woodall has written and edited for literary magazines in the past, and this, his first novel, is intended for those with a love of high fantasy in the tradition of Narnia and Middle Earth. Mr. Woodall lives in western Arkansas.

CPSIA information can be obtained at www.ICGtesting.com
Printed in the USA
LVOW080234211011

251458LV00001B/15/P